A Defense of Poetry

MW01146854

Collected works

Andrew Nightingale 2019

ISBN 9781688505711
Published by Trial by Fire

365/1338 Putta Bucha Soi 47
Bangmod Thungkru
Bangkok 10140

Visit www.questionsarepower.org

ACKNOWLEDGEMENTS

The success of these works depended on support from my father Dr. Kevin G Barnhurst, my mother Lucinda A Nightingale, my wife Nannapat R Nightingale and daughters Alina L Nightingale and Evelyn W Nightingale. My step-fathers Dr. Richard Doherty and Khabir Leclaire, my brother Dr. Matthew Barnhurst and sister Clara Barnhurst. This is my family, my debt to them will probably never be clearly understood until the last moments of my life.

I have had many teachers in my life, but my lifetime mentor Dr. Alejandro Medina introduced me to the concept of vagueness, 10 years before this book. I owe a deep debt of gratitude to him for his hand in waking me up. There are also the Thai Buddhist monks, most especially Master Ratana at the monastery in Chicago, and Ven. Samrit at the monastery in Chumponburi, Surin, Thailand. Other teachers who played very important roles in my life are Dr. Tim McLarnan as an undergraduate, who introduced me to non-Euclidean Geometry, and Dr. Martin Buntinas, who guided me through my M.S. in mathematics, and once said "Mathematics is the poetry of the sciences."

I also would like to thank Dr. Parames Laosinchai, for his kind attention and interest, helpful feedback and general support. Also Dr. Khajornsak Buaraphan lent his support in important ways to this project. I would also like to thank Dr Paul Ernest for his feedback. The reviewers at Teaching Philosophy helped to improve the essay on the Pedagogy of Logical Pluralism.

Finally I would like to thank the Waldorf School San Sanook for allowing me to conduct research there. It was quite difficult to find schools willing to participate. After receiving some rejections, one that openly denied that paraconsistent logic was valid, another that refused to give a reason why they would not allow the study to happpen at their school, I began to suspect that multiple logics was not a topic that school officials welcomed. So, I thank the school head of San Sanook (Mrs. Reywadee) for her vision in allowing her school to be the site for the study of vagueness.

Andrew Nightingale

Table of Contents

The Pedagogy of Logical Pluralism

ABSTRACT

This paper makes an original rhetorical contribution about the nature of logical negation. Following Peirce (1933), who reduced classical logic to its negation operation—distinction—this paper offers that negation should be presented as the central concept of logic for its pedagogical value. This is somewhat different from the prevailing view that logical consequence is the central topic of logic. Vagueness of logical consequence is the "common" reason (Gillian 2019) to assert logical pluralism. Logical negation can have other meanings (Wittgenstein 1976), and here it is offered that logical negation is vague, which leads to logical pluralism as well. Logical pluralism gained salience in recent years in academic circles, beginning with Beall & Restall's work culminating in a book (2006). There is now a large variety of logics cropping up. As a secondary part of the paper, a web app program called "Logic Puzzle," coded by the author, aimed to make the abstract conceptual work about logical negation and vagueness more specific and concrete, and allows visual comparison between different logical negation operations. This program could be used in late high school math classes, though perhaps it is more appropriate for undergraduate math education classes. Finally, a preliminary empirical study combining qualitative and quantitative methods was conducted with the triangulable result that the technology increased awareness of choice in mathematics. Any curriculum modifications are left for the teachers to develop.

Keywords: Logical Pluralism, Education, Philosophy of Mathematics, Educational Technology, Vagueness

Background

Logical pluralism is the view that there is more than one correct deductive logic, or way to sharpen the concept of logical consequence (the "if, then"), and gained prominence in academic circles recently. Since a number of papers by Beall and Restall, culminating in a book (2006), many other kinds of logic cropped up (Gillian 2019). Differing ones include Varzi (2002) who adds more logical constants than other logicians do, Russell (2008) offers another logical pluralism between truth-bearers (the entities that can bear a truth-like property) such as sentences and propositions. Then there are varieties of logical pluralism holding that logics are models of language (Shapiro 2006; Cook 2010; Shapiro 2014), with the correct logic changing according to your goal or reason for modeling. The Stoics began logical pluralism, in a sense, in the variety of views that arose in their debates on logical consequence (Mates, 1961). Carnap upheld a particular kind of pluralism (Carnap 1937) that could be practiced by changing the language, the "syntactical rules" and "methods" (Ibid. §17).

Lakatos argued (1962) that logic is traditionally used to justify many branches of knowledge, starting with definitions and "proving" the rest, following the Euclidean form. Euclid's axiomatic form is historically very important for teaching. For thousands of years, Euclid's books have been important textbooks, and, after the Renaissance, they are the most widely read textbooks in the world. (Hartshorne 2000, p1) Euclid's innovation was not geometry but the form of proving propositions using classical logic, based on simple axioms. When non-Euclidean geometry was discovered, doubt was cast, not just on Euclidean geometry as true, but Euclid's axiomatic form based on classical logic.

The change from classical logic to logical pluralism is a fundamental one. Not only is it gaining salience in academia, the shift portends a reorganization of many branches of knowledge, adding other valid ways to justify knowledge (while not subtracting the already "Euclidean" forms of knowledge). The prominence of logical pluralism leaves an opening to discover another fundamental way of teaching and presenting logic, different from Euclid's. Logical pluralism changes the landscape of scholarship, the teacher's curriculum, and of course the student's understanding of mathematics in a fundamental way.

A firm reason for logical pluralism involves the recognition of probability as a fuzzy logic, a logic that is not simply used, but asserted as objects that exist in quantum physics.

> ...probability theory might provide a canon for evaluating degrees of belief, ... Nonetheless, probability theory cannot be a complete answer here, for... In particular, we hold that it is a mistake to assert the premises of a valid argument while denying the conclusion...(Beall & Restall 2006: loc 292)

Statistical reasoning allows a null hypothesis to be rejected based on a probability. This shows how two logics – a two-valued accept/reject logic, and an uncountably-many-valued fuzzy logic – are joined.

The goal of this paper is to offer a pedagogy of logical pluralism that can be appropriate for high school teachers to understand and adapt for high school education. As such it is addressed to people who know classical logic well, and begins the long journey from classical logic to poetry. [Note: If you are more interested in vagueness or poetry, skip to the middle or end of the book] When adapting a topic for pedagogy, the concepts have to change into something rhetorically easy to accept. The basic pedagogical idea is a didactic between vagueness and the logical negation operation – distinction. Russell (1923) and Shapiro (2008, Loc 988-995) argued that vagueness is the opposite of distinction, and thus what vagueness is, exactly, must be left indistinct.

Beall and Restall argued that logical pluralism in one language was made possible by the vague logical consequence symbol, the "if, then." "the concept of logical consequence is not sharp." (Beall & Restall 2006 Kindle Locations 111-112) "there are different but mutually compatible and equally legitimate ways to sharpen or further articulate the intuitive notion(s) of logical consequence and validity." (Shapiro 2014, p1-2) While the term vagueness seems carefully avoided, it is latent in these descriptions of logical consequence; logical consequence(s) are "not sharp" because they are vague. It was also explicitly stated that logical consequence is vague by Tarskey (1956, p409). Gillian (2019) explicitly stated that the "common" argument for logical pluralism is the vagueness of logical consequence. With these four authorities, I will continue with the assumption that vagueness is a central problem of logic (if not *the* central problem of logic) that creates the opportunity for logical pluralism.

This paper puts forth the idea that negation is the fundamental operation of logic, which is somewhat different from the prevailing view that logical consequence is the fundamental operation of logic. Logical pluralism, or recognizing different logics, are a matter of recognizing differing logical consequences, according to the common view. Peirce wanted to reduce logic to a single symbol for logical consequence, but what he succeeded in doing was reducing logic to negation. (Peirce 1933) Peirce's result is still a success in simplifying logic(s). This simplification is the reasoning behind the claim offered here that recognizing different logics is a matter of recognizing *distinct kinds of distinction.*

The Contribution: Distinct Kinds of Distinction

Peirce defined vagueness in terms of the law of non-contradiction, which is an exercise in applying the classical negation operation: $\sim\sim P \to P$. Peirce says that we are in a vague situation when this law fails to be true. (Peirce 1960, 505). The law of non-contradiction can take different forms. The modern form, the one used in proof by contradiction, is $\sim\sim P \to P$. Pluralism is possible when "not-not-P" does not mean "P," instead it means a distinct kind of "not-P," or a different way of negating P. For example, most people with a drive to avoid vagueness can easily agree that a neutron star is different from a question *in a different way* from how a lemon is different from a lime. However, agreeing to distinct kinds of distinctions (call these distinctions "A") makes the law of non-contradiction fail, and puts people trying to avoid vagueness into vague territory.

One may say that having different ways of negating P does not indicate an indistinctness, it indicates greater distinctness. This depends on how we use the word distinctness. First of all, with the idea of "greater distinctness" we have already shifted our use of mere distinctness, to an undefined idea of *degrees* of distinctness, which implies a vagueness of our use of distinctness. Further, suppose there were type A distinctions between the same thing – for example, a right isosceles triangle with two equal sides measuring 1cm (call this triangle x) and a square with sides of 1cm (called y). x and y are different in that one has 3 sides and the other has 4. They are also different in that x is one triangle, and y is two x triangles put together. To simply call the triangle and the square distinct is to be vague on how they are distinct. The claim here is that is exactly what we do, and because of this, distinctness is indistinct/vague. We are not being precise about our kinds of distinctions.

There are many attempts to solve vagueness. One attempt is to argue that we *could* find all the precisifications of a given vague use of the word distinction, and it makes no difference if we use distinction for all these distinctions for the sake of economy. To counter, suppose for example we want to find exactly where the end of my nose is (this is a common example of the problem of vagueness). We want to be very precise about all the parts of the line that distinguish my nose from not-my-nose, so we magnify. Unfortunately, this magnification makes the line harder and harder to describe, and eventually we get into quantum physics and can't find the line anymore. The vagueness of distinction is just like any other vagueness, it can't be solved by being more precise. In looking for all the distinctions between distinctions we will become unsure of whether they are distinctions at all (see the section "On Vagueness" below). However, we *can* be sure of *some* distinctions between distinctions (as in distinction "A" above).

There are different ways to make the negation operation precise. The negation or distinction is not universal, but classical logical negation attempts to be universal, and the defining characteristic of classical logic negation is that $\sim\sim P$ implies P. The only way this can be true is if there is only one kind of negation operation, and it is universal/absolute. If the first "$\sim$" in "$\sim\sim P$" means one thing and the second "$\sim$" means another, we don't know if we have P, or another kind of "$\sim P$." Wittgenstein (1976, p 80) already argued that there are other ways logical negation can be used. In his example, in effect a second negation on top of the first doesn't do anything except add emphasis to a single negation. Here it is offered that a double negation can have many logical significances beyond mere emphasis, and beyond the total reversal of classical logical negation. The actual differences between differences, or logical negation operations, observed here are being brought to their natural conclusion: that the concept of difference is vague.

Derrida recognized one kind of distinction, different from the mathematical understanding of difference as a kind of absolute, unqualified ideal. It may be that Derrida's differance is a conflation of the absolute difference/not-equals of mathematics, with the idea of meaning being deferred. It may also be that the connotation of deferred in diferance is a qualification that makes diferance more precise than difference. Either way, the reason difference can be qualified is that the idea of difference as an unqualified absolute suffers from vagueness, that any observed difference is already conflated with other differences. And this vagueness is natural, in the same way that there are natural kinds, there is a natural failure to classify, to name. As in measuring the plank of wood, the length is never perfectly measured. The idea that there is an "actual" length "out there," or that the ultimate meaning (in the correspondence sense) of a length of a wooden plank is deferred to the completion of a never-ending measurement task is contrasted with the idea that the "actual" length is naturally vague, and the task need not be completed. For finite beings, all measurements are vague (people tend to call this "error", but error implies that the vagueness people encounter is essentially unreal, even though it is encountered constantly whether we use precise measuring tools or our human senses). Derrida's diferance is not the negation or difference operation in constructive logic, or the paraconsistent definition of negation in Costa's C1 (1977), or the many other formulations of the logical negation axiom, and these are all different from the absolute mathematical not-equals, and classical logical negation.

What is the significance for philosophy of math? There are two ways to handle the recognition that distinctness in its present form is indistinct. One way is to introduce new words for different kinds of distinctness, or make standard the use of qualifying words for this difference or that difference. This path would change the mathematical use of the not-equals symbol and the negation operation, and make logical pluralism standard. Another way to handle it is to accept that vagueness is not something we can avoid by pursuing a never-ending task of refining language. I am in favor of the second path – one of embracing vagueness. Ullman (1970) has a section called "Words with blurred edges" (1970, p 116) where he notices that vagueness is seen as a strength by poets, but seen as a bad thing by natural philosophers (the old name for scientists). Speaking as a published poet, my experience of education in the USA did not favor the poet's temperament to embrace vagueness. To trouble the first path of handling the indistinctness of distinctness, it could be pointed out that there are higher-order varieties of the same problem of distinctions between distinctions – that there can be distinctions between the distinctions between distinctions, etc. and these would lead us back into a realm where vagueness must be accepted as, if not real and good, as constantly present in everyday life and troubling attempts to make distinctions. Distinction is problematic; higher-order distinction is not any less problematic than higher-order vagueness – the problem that solutions to vagueness are themselves vague.

There is no reason to privilege distinctness over vagueness, as Feyerabend (1975) argued that there is no reason to privilege the telescope over the naked eye. In this, the ideas here place themselves under ancient skepticism, not nihilism nor relativism. Ancient skepticism guards a person against turning their sense impression into dogma that is not immediately apparent. (Empírico, S., & Mates, B. 1996) The impressions the senses make to you are not open to question. This is not to say that knowledge is impossible, but simply that knowledge found in poetry "weighs in" just as much as knowledge found in the sciences.

In Verlaine (1884, p23-25):

> Rien de plus cher que la chanson
> grise Où l'Indécis au Précis se joint.

l'Indécis can be translated as vagueness and Précis as precision, "Nothing is more valuable than the grey song where vagueness and precision join."

In Nightingale (2018) a study of teaching vagueness found that students who were perceived as "bad" or uncooperative were the most engaged and pro-active when the topic of empirical investigation was vagueness. This seems to indicate that education in what Nightingale coined as "precision knowledge" is hostile to certain temperaments. There are further social effects to the pursuit of "precision knowledge" in mathematics, and sciences who follow mathematical reasoning. Precision knowledge has a divisive effect on people and discourse, as is illustrated in the story of the Tower of Babel.

On Vagueness

There is too much to say about the many attempts to define vagueness. For this paper, we have adopted Peirce's definition of vagueness, as the failure of the law of noncontradiction. However, Peirce made this definition when only one logic was recognized. For vagueness to take on its role in logical pluralism, the concept of vagueness was repurposed in Nightingale (2018). In general, the description of vagueness is better left to poetry. Rowland (2000) offered that the "question" itself is an expression of vagueness. If that is the case, describing vagueness would be a description of everything we can inquire about. The most "complete" attempt at doing this, outside the field of poetry, would be in real number analysis, although it is argued in Nightingale (2013) that this attempt, while beautiful to some, still fails.

Wandering among different definitions (vague comes from the Latin vagus which means to wander), the roads seemed to converge to Russell's definition of vagueness, when a word leads its user towards more than one applicable meaning...language is a "garden of forking paths" to quote Borge's story about a book that actually succeeds in chronicling the passage of time, forking as all possible choices are made. Russell noticed that these paths can be seen in experience—as things come closer, a multitude of details become available, all calling us to follow them. Sometimes I refer to this "general law of physics" (Russell 1923) as vagueness, ... in the case when you are looking at a star in the sky through a telescope, and you can almost make out that it looks like two stars close together, we can say that "that light is one star" or "that light is two stars". Holding both these statements is classically illogical by noncontradiction, and both can be held because the situation is vague—both in Peirce's sense and Russell's physical law. (Nightingale 2018, p 21-22)

Whatever vagueness is, the borderline case is the where vagueness has made the most trouble for logicians. For example, Shapiro (2008) describes the borderline case with imagining an array of 2000 men from entirely bald on one side and gradually (imperceptibly, even) changing to a very hairy Jerry Garcia on the other end of the array. He attacks this ancient problem with what he calls the "forced march," done by a group of "competent" speakers. They start with Jerry Garcia and investigate the next man, reaching a consensus each time, and the inference "if n is not bald, then n+1 is not bald" appears valid. Shapiro is concerned with the eventuality that the inference will break down and the competent speakers will be filled with conflict until they decide that one of the men is bald. This is because the difference between the words "bald" and "not bald" are vague, or there are cases where the word bald can be applied to a man that is arguably bald or not bald, if inquiry becomes more sensitive. This is how the borderline case relates to our definitions of vagueness in the previous paragraph.

The "competent speakers" or "masters" of meaning[1] decide man n is bald when they had just agreed man n-1 was not bald. Shapiro seems to say that the speakers can stop there, even though, as Shapiro mentions, the competent speakers will be aware that the same change or jump at n from not bald to bald spreads to some indeterminate n-k other people who were previously validly inferred to be not bald and are now bald, because the change from n-1 to n is imperceptible to the naked eye (a similar example of vagueness can be produced regardless of the power of the microscope or telescope; regardless of the sensitivity of any scientific instrument). If the purpose of the conversation were to figure out who was bald and who wasn't, wouldn't the speakers turn back and start inferring that n-1 is bald, etc and etc? Since Shapiro chooses classical logic "without argument" (Shapiro. 2008, Kindle Location 1023,) and classical logic requires the Law of Excluded Middle, the target of conversation is necessarily settled "out there." To know where (and if) this is settled, the speakers would have to enter into a never-ending conversation. Facing vagueness between bald and not bald, the committee has a choice to deliberate on a vague situation forever, or allow classical logic to come into question. Here Shapiro upholds a latent ideal of *work* as a saving power against contradiction, but that power only saves as long as work continues, and returns to contradiction if the "masters" give up.

Nightingale (2018) put forth the idea that vagueness is a material part of inquiry. When inquiring into the length of a wooden plank, one takes centimeters, then millimeters, etc, but ultimately the measuring tool fails to take the "actual" length of the plank – the body of the plank is vague (Nightingale 2013). Dewey defended the thesis that logic arises from inquiry. "the view here expressed, they (logical laws) represent conditions which have been ascertained during the conduct of continued inquiry to be involved in its own successful pursuit." (Dewey 1938 Loc 284-286).

---

[1] As Shapiro puts it, I am sure he counts himself as one of these "masters"

Inquiry with the senses, as has long been recognized, is fraught with vagueness. Vagueness and logic are complementary; they are part of the same activity: inquiry. Vagueness is when reality spills over out of our word-containers in the chase and capture of reality with words, or it is what escapes us when involved in any inquiry.

Probability is often misunderstood as a solution to vagueness, and without vagueness, there is no reason to assert logical pluralism. The way probability deals with vagueness is by giving vague situations real-valued *degrees* between opposites.

> 'One serious objection ... is that it really replaces vagueness with the most refined and incredible precision. Set membership, as viewed by the degrees of truth theorist, comes in precise degrees, ... The result is a commitment to precise dividing lines that is not only unbelievable but also thoroughly contrary to what I [call] "robust" or "resilient" vagueness. For ... it seems an essential part of the resilient vagueness of ordinary terms such as "bald", "tall", and "overweight" that in Sorites sequences ... there is indeterminacy with respect to the division between the conditionals that have the value 1, and those that have the next highest value, whatever it might be. It is this central feature of vagueness which the degrees of truth approach, in its standard form, fails to accommodate, regardless of how many truth-values it introduces'. "(Tye 1994: p 14)

The measurement of the wooden plank is a good example of why vagueness persists in the face of the theory of real numbers, because the progression of measurement can be seen as an infinite and bounded sequence, which allows it to fall under the definition of the axiom of completeness: the property that distinguishes the real numbers from other numbers (Abbot 2001). It has already been argued elsewhere that this property fails in answering the problem of vagueness (Nightingale 2018, Nightingale 2013).

With this philosophical contribution outlined, the paper takes the path of recognizing distinctions between distinctions, and making them clear to students. A computer program called "Logic Puzzle" was written by the author with the intent of introducing various negation operations to high school students and prospective math teachers, and is presented here to show how the abstract argument above can be made concrete and coded into a technology. The program was used by high school and undergraduate students, and their responses were studied using a combination of qualitative and quantitative methods. The philosophical contribution just outlined is then incorporated into the empirical findings as a conclusion.

Introducing "Logic Puzzle"

The idea that there is more than one way to make the negation operation precise, and thus that the negation operation is vague, was coded into a computer program by the author to allow a more specific, concrete presentation of the abstract conceptual work done above. The web app program "Logic Puzzle" could be used to instruct undergraduate math, math education, or late high school students. It involves fitting puzzle pieces together to create logical statements. There are three settings: classical, paraconsistent, and constructive logic. The program automatically generates the logical statement in normal notation, along with graphs of classical logic, paraconsistent truth tables, and separate graphs for the constructive logic setting.

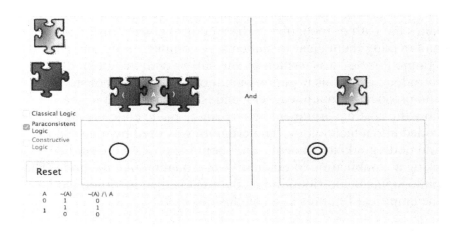

Figure 1: Peircian logic graphs (the circles) with paraconsistent truth tables (on the bottom left).

A user can mouse over puzzle pieces, graphs and truth tables to get a description of each object. To build a logical statement, one merely drags-and-drops puzzle pieces in ways they fit together. If you would like to play with Logic Puzzle, go to http://159.89.203.232/LogicPuzzle-Dev/.

When a green piece is dragged to the right place, it modifies the logical statement by adding a proposition labeled "A," "B," or "C." When a blue puzzle piece is dragged to the right place, it acts as both the parenthesis and the negation operation, so a left and a right blue piece is needed to close the parenthesis and indicate what is being negated. There are two possible instances of "A," "B," or "C." one on the left and one on the right (in the picture) this creates the possibility of building two statements with puzzle pieces that are in contradiction. When a user builds a contradiction, the program asks about changing to paraconsistent logic, and draws a paraconsistent truth table under the Peircian graphs.

Classical Logic Setting

The Peircian graphs (Peirce 1933) reduce logic to a single symbol: the circle. The circle notation distinguishes between its inside and outside, it is effectively the negation operation. The Peircian graphs suggest a way of using space, or a lack of notation, instead of the AND operation.

Here is an example

Figure 2

This symbol is equivalent to "~(A AND ~B)", since the outside circle suggests an A on the left, and a ~B on the right of its inside. This symbol is equivalent to "If A, then B". It may be noticed that there is a "latent" symbol in use here because the ellipse also suggests the use of the operation AND. One may say that this notation is only possible with a loose definition of "circle" that includes ellipses. Nightingale introduces a new notation for Peirce's graphs that has the same effect but there is no variation in the basic symbol.

> The mark required for the spirit of the Peircian graph is so elemental it is almost simply the requirement that any mark be written. So:
>
> ! | ||
>
> Can be the same symbol as the Peircian circles above, the first and last mark begins and ends the outer ellipse, and the middle two marks are "~B". Putting the last two lines as close together as possible makes the meaning of this notation more or less unambiguous. However, all notation is ambiguous, including classical logic notation. (Nightingale 2018, p 42-43)

Space is the site for joining things together with "and.".
Foucault eloquently described the rupture between "language," or
notation, and "space." He quotes Borges (2002), who writes about
an ancient Chinese Encyclopedia that attempts to enumerate the
world. Among the enumerations are (In Foucault 1973):

> The animals "(i) frenzied, (j) innumerable, (k) drawn
> with a very fine camelhair brush"— where could they
> ever meet...? Where else could they be juxtaposed except
> in the non-place of language? Yet, though language can
> spread them before us, it can do so only in an
> unthinkable space. The central category of animals
> "included in the present classification", with its explicit
> reference to paradoxes we are familiar with, is indication
> enough that we shall never succeed in defining a stable
> relation of contained to container... Absurdity destroys
> the *and* of the enumeration by making impossible the *in*
> where the things enumerated would be divided up."
> (Foucault 1973, xvi-xvii)

The space in a Peircian graph shows how, before Borges,
language "intersected space." While Russell's Paradox made
explicit the paradox of set theory (of the relationship between
container and contained), the logical pluralist would not
immediately reject set theory (or the contents of Peircian circles)
on that counter-example, but would use set theory for situations
where the paradox does not arise, and invent a new or discover
an old logic to handle the paradox when it arises.The linguistic
"and" and the spacial "in" can be linked again, if we allow
vagueness to permeate space, instead of the traditional set-
theoretic definition of real-numbers as a model for space. In any
case, such a conception of space allows logical notation to be
reduced to the negation symbol. It is the purpose of the program
"logic puzzle" is to teach negation as the fundamental idea of
logic, and that this fundamental idea has more than one form.
There are "different kinds of negation" That is the pedagogical
approach of the logic puzzle.

Paraconsistent Logic Setting

The paraconsistent logic chosen supports the idea that negation is the fundamental idea in logic. Costa's C1 (1977) is defined by allowing a new line in the truth table anytime something true (represented with a "1" in the truth table above) is negated in another column in the truth table, the new line allows the negation to be true ("1"), while the old line will be the expected "false" ("0") value. So we have a situation where if A is true, ~A may be true or false, and the law of excluded middle (That "out there" or for external reality, it must be decided whether A or ~A, not both) fails. Moving from the Peircian graphs that reduce classical logic to negation, this particular paraconsistent logic is entirely defined by a difference in the definition of negation, emphasizing the importance of negation (or distinction) as the fundamental operation of logic.

Constructive Logic Setting

The constructive logic setting is similar in that you build statements the same way, by dragging and dropping puzzle pieces. There are green pieces that are the "propositions" or constructions and the same blue piece for both negation and parenthesis. The meaning of "A," "B," or "C." is explained, so "A" is a connected ring, "B" is a star-shape with rays coming from a central point, and "C" is a "mesh" This is because the "truth-value" of a constructive logic statement is not "true," but "constructed" and this makes negation calculate differently.

The possibilities are: 1) A or a ring is constructed, if that is all the user has built by dragging and dropping a green puzzle piece, then the graph will be a picture of a connected ring of nodes. 2) if ~A is constructed with puzzle pieces, the graph will show a configuration of nodes that makes it impossible to connect them into a ring. 3) If ~~A is constructed with puzzle pieces, the graph will show a configuration of unconnected nodes where it is possible to connect them into a ring, e.g. "A is constructable but not constructed," if "A and B" is constructed, there will be nodes in a ring, and the nodes will also be connected in a way that forms a star shape (see picture below for "A and B"). Negation has yet another fundamental difference in constructive logic. Starting with "constructed" (A), "not constructed (and constructable)" is (~~A) and "not constructable" is (~A).

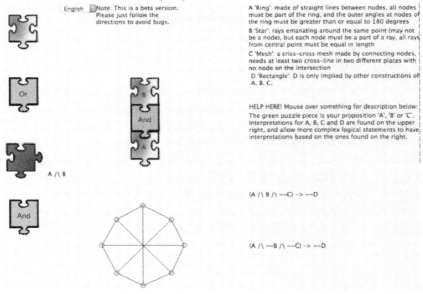

Figure 3: Constructive Logic Setting; "A AND B"

The pedagogy presented by the "Logic Puzzle" program should be understandable to undergraduate students in math or math education. While all these concepts may not be explicitly learned by high-school students using the logic puzzle, the intent is that students will be exposed, or immersed, in a teaching tool with an important message: there are different logics, these logics are defined by their differing negation operations, and these differences can be compared, side by side, within a technological setting. The pedagogy of logical pluralism can be felt by students, even if they do not master the teachers' understanding presented here, compressed as it is from the wider context available to a scholar. It is often the case that mathematical arguments are not made to young students, such as the argument for real numbers, as numbers, or as real.

The argument for real numbers isn't presented fully unless a student majors in mathematics in college, where a student can find at the very end (covered?) of an undergraduate text on real numbers: "We all grow up believing in the existence of real numbers, but it is only through study of classical analysis that we become aware of their elusive and enigmatic nature." (Abbott 2001, p 244) Unfortunately for many students, such arguments are often not of much help. This is one purpose of making "Logic Puzzle;" it presents an important mathematical idea with automatic graph generation, help messages as needed, and the mathematical rigor calculated "under the hood." With the pedagogy of logical pluralism and its conception of the program "Logic Puzzle" explained, we will turn to how the logic puzzle application is to be studied, then to exactly what the students are able to grasp using this tool.

Methodology

> ..the field indicated, that of inquiries, is already pre-empted. There is, it will be said, a recognized subject which deals with it. That subject is methodology; and there is a well recognized distinction between methodology and logic, the former being an application of the latter." (Dewey 1938 Loc 166-168)

Dewey writes that the reason methodology and logic are seen as separate is logic is needed as an external and certain standard to judge methods of scientific inquiry.

> How can inquiry originate logical forms (as it has been stated that it does) and yet be subject to the requirements of these forms?" [Dewey 1938 Loc 179-180]
> The problem reduced to its lowest terms is whether inquiry can develop in its own ongoing course the logical standards and forms to which further inquiry shall submit. One might reply by saying that it can because it has. One might even challenge the objector to produce a single instance of improvement in scientific methods not produced in and by the self-corrective process of inquiry;" (Dewey 1938 Loc 182-185)

How does one make assumptions about a methodology when the standard of judging methodologies are under scrutiny? This is why a qualitative approach is preferred. Induction is a very different logic from the deductive logics being examined. The study in quires using Grounded theory (Glaser & Strauss 1967) because there is no literature on logical pluralism, or the comparison between multiple deductive logics, as a topic of empirical study in education, except Nightingale (2018).

There were three instruments to the Logic Puzzle: a pre-post attitudinal survey (quantitative), a worksheet that guides the students to try certain constructions in classical, paraconsistent, and constructive logic, asking for their feedback (qualitative), and a post test asking them to select a logic given a situation. The test was partially quantitative and partially qualitative, with a correct answer of which logic, and any information the student felt they wanted to add.

The worksheet instructed the students to construct the statement "A and ~A," a contradiction, so that Logic Puzzle drew Peircian graphs and a paraconsistent truth table. The students were then asked questions like what the graphs mean, how classical Peircian and constructive graphs differ, about how classical logic truth tables and paraconsistent truth tables are different. At the end there were open ended questions about what they thought about the program.

Logical pluralism introduced to students with the Web App called "Logic Puzzle" was in one language: Thai. In Thailand, Western (The usual truth-table classical logic) logic has colonized the national curriculum, and teachers begin instruction of logic to students around age 16. However, a requirement throughout the mathematics curriculum is "suitable reasoning". With this requirement, education authorities in Thailand present mathematics as the model for how students should reason.

The students were generally college and late high school students in front of a computer doing an investigation into logic, not for fun. The worksheet-style direction and feedback part were coded and then the codes were investigated using basic qualitative questioning. The codes were compared to further define them and their relationships to each other to better understand the students experience of Logic Puzzle. Certain words were selected for meaning exploration. The quantitative results are the most tentative form of research applied in this study, because probability is under scrutiny.

Data and Results

Qualitative findings:

Because there were only 7 subjects in this study, the presentation of data can be more fine-grained; 10 worksheet questions makes 70 answers in the worksheet. There were a small number of coded "insightful answers" (8/70) that go beyond these types of merely "correct" (28/70) answers. Outside the two questions that almost nobody understood (what is a contradiction and how are the constructive and classical graphs alike/different) there were 7 misunderstand/blank. Having a graph gave students a visual to connect to the definition of negation. Maybe this contributed to the idea that the tool (or logical pluralism?) "made it easier" (5/70)

"Choice" (6/70) was another code. Students are generally not given a choice about mathematical facts. Giving students choices helps them to see that whatever math fact they are looking at was a choice made by mathematicians, not an absolute truth. They do not have to accept them or "hang on a word" or symbol. Students can think more freely because mathematics is seen as more hypothetical. There was indication that giving students choices "made it easier", there was no indication that giving students choices in math made things harder. Another student sees that a different logic has the potential to be more concrete (constructive), instead of more general(paraconsistent).

"Relates to everyday life" (2/70) was another code. It was strange to see this code at all. I did not expect that students would be able to relate abstract A's and B's, logical operations, and geometrical graphs to everyday life. "Paraconsistent logic is possible with 2 answers. Can be used in everyday life more than Classical logic" Here we see a connection made by a student between choice (having possible answers) and everyday life. Is math seen as difficult simply because it is asserted as without choice, unlike life?

Quantitative results

For the attitudinal questionnaire, because of the small sample size, only large effect sizes were tested using a matched pair, one-tailed Student's t-test. There were three questions (out of 12 in the survey) with a large Cohen's D effect size (approx .89); two of these questions had interesting statistical significance. The first was "If I have a thought that is not mathematical, I know that it is not worthwhile." This changed from being neutral and agreeing somewhat, to leaning towards disagreeing after the activity. The statistical significance of this large and important effect size, was $p = .051$. While this is technically not a significant finding, in a strict orthodox view, it is still a tantalizing finding that indicates a fruitful direction for further study, especially given the small sample size of 7.

The next question was "Mathematics is not important in everyday life." This also changed from neutral and somewhat agreeing, to somewhat disagreeing. The Cohen's D effect size was large (.89) so a t-test was conducted and a p value of $p = .52$ was found. Another interesting, if unorthodox finding. It is the author's view that if schools had allowed logical pluralism into their classrooms so that a large sample size would have been available, there would be a significant finding that the logical pluralism activity helped students to see a relationship between logic and everyday life.

Summary of findings

The strongest result—that of having a choice—is found in the test, the survey (more thoughts are worthwhile), and the worksheet, so it is triangulated. Emphatically, the choices given to students in Logic Puzzle are epistemologically fundamental. They are not trivial choices about how to express the same answer, or different ways of getting essentially the same answer. These are *real* choices. There was no indication that having possibilities made things harder, but there was indication that having possibilities made things easier.

Insightful students noticed that the paraconsistent truth table is "Different with many more meanings than traditional [logic]." or "Rejection[negation] in constructive logic can be done in two ways, but for classical logic there is only one way" in response to how classical logic is different from constructive logic. This is the main pedagogical message of Logic Puzzle: that there are choices of logics because of distinctions between kinds of negation.

Conclusion

Students found more options with logical pluralism, and that comes as no surprise. They felt this freedom as a connection to life, and a sense of ease. Math could have been done in a different way, and its not as if traditional math does not have contradictions (Weber N.D.). It is supposed that students can feel this, even if they don't know it – in the same way that real numbers are commonly presented intuitively without precise, mathematically rigorous arguments.

The message of Logic Puzzle as a technology "endowed or entrusted with meaning" (Latour 2002, p 29) is that logical deduction is not final. The fact that there is a variety of logics bends the blade of distinction against itself, rendering traditional taxonomies and bodies of knowledge dependent on an absolute idea of distinction open to question. And with honest inquiry there is an opening for constructing new meanings, finding new patterns and for new readings of ancient texts.

It has been observed that "the question" is how to express vagueness (Rowland 2000), and logical pluralism, as a response to the vague concept of logical negation, evokes questions more easily than classical logic alone, which presents itself as final.

The logic (with probability presented as a "theory" not a logic) in Thai schools today is consistent with the Law of Excluded Middle: that there is no real question whether it is A or ~A, "out there," this question is always settled. With Excluded Middle vagueness is unreal or error, and the reality is a world of external answers, already settled "out there." (Brouwer 1981) Classical logic puts learners in situations where they have to deal with contradictions, such as the indistinctness of distinctness, and does not teach them a freedom of thought that allows them to deal with contradictions. One example is instantaneous velocity, which is a contradiction in terms. It is better to not assert that such a concept is precise *and* in contradiction; rather, instantaneous velocity is vague and that is why the law of non-contradiction fails. "How can an object have velocity if it doesn't have time to move?" This is how to think about instantaneous velocity. Firstly, asking a question about a contradiction just feels better to students than compelling them to accept something conflicting. Secondly a question has the property of being neither true nor false, which is the kind of proposition you need for a contradiction. A real question is one that is particularly stubborn and keeps coming up after generations of trying to answer it. Motion, consciousness and vagueness are examples of real questions.

With logical pluralism, teachers can show students a rejection of the logical terms used to create the contradiction, not in a negative way, but by introducing new logical terms in other logics. So instantaneous velocity uses the mathematical construct of points to describe movement. Rejection of the logical objects used to describe movement does not reject the question about movement, but leads to looking for other logics to ask about it.

Even if logical pluralism is not adopted in a curriculum, teachers ought to give their students permission to reject contradictions, and how would they do that safely without giving them alternative logical negation operations, allowing the failure of the law of noncontradiction by giving alternatives? Compelling assent to a contradiction without alternatives is the opposite of education. On the other hand, appealing to unending inquiry can be paralyzing and equally unhelpful. Introducing a variety of logics is a middle-ground solution, allowing students to articulate their questions with respect to a particular logic, and adapt to contradictions by recognizing that any logic has vague aspects.

There is no intent here to endorse the idea that anything can be true. Maybe a limited relativism is supported because absolutism is rejected as a result of the honest recognition that the logical negation operation is vague. People still need (vague) interaction, and have (vague) standards of reasoning to judge and believe ideas and writing. The perspective of logical pluralism is that there are many deductive standards to use, and perhaps some yet uninvented. Relativism isn't really a serious point of view because logical standards, conversations, ideologies, paradigms, cultures, etc are vague. The idea that something can be relatively true from from the point of view of a culture or something else requires that this culture be fully defined the way classical logic is believed to be. Unfortunately, classical logic is not fully defined, nor is any culture or anything else (this is a direct result of the indistinctness of distinctness). Neither does this mean nothing is true. Ancient skepticism asserts that sense impressions are true and not open to question, even though they are vague, so nihilism is rejected.

Science education focuses on teaching a precise concept, even in alternative approaches like Philosophy for Children (P4C) (Ferriera 2012). However, vagueness is more interesting to students (Nightingale 2018), and pluralism helps understanding, against the idea that there is a scientific "true/real" precise concept, without contending concepts. The latent ideal of *work* that Shapiro upholds as a saving power against contradiction is contrasted with an ideal of *rest*, offered in Pyrrhonism as Ataraxia, because vagueness is found both after tremendous amounts of work and investigation using big science apparatus, as well as without work, immediately to our human senses.

REFERENCES

Beall, J., & Restall, G. (2006). *Logical pluralism*. Oxford: Clarendon Press ;.

Borges, J. L. (2002). *Other inquisitions: 1937-1952*. Austin: University of Texas Press.

Brouwer, L. E., & Dalen, D. V. (1981). *Brouwer's Cambridge lectures on intuitionism*. Cambridge: Cambridge University Press.

Brouwer, L. E. J. (1907). *On the Foundations of Mathematics* Thesis, Amsterdam; English translation in Heyting (ed.) 1975: 11–101.

Brouwer, L. E. J. (1908). *The Unreliability of the Logical Principles* English translation in Heyting (ed.) 1975: 107–111.

Carnap, R. (1937). THE LOGICAL SYNTAX OF LANGUAGE. London: Kegan Paul.

Dewey, J. (1938). *Logic, the theory of inquiry*. New York: H. Holt and Company.

Drago, A. (2018). Suggestion for Teaching Science as a Pluralist Enterprise. *Transversal: International   Journal for the Historiography of Science,* (5), 66. doi:10.24117/2526-2270.2018.i5.07

Feyerabend, P. (2010). *Against method.* London: Verso.

Foucault, M. (1973). *The order of things: An archaeology of the human sciences.* New York: Vintage Books.

Cook, R., 2010, "Let a thousand flowers bloom: a tour of logical pluralism," PHILOSOPHY COMPASS, 5(6): 492–504.

Corbin, J. M., & Strauss, A. L. (2015). *Basics of qualitativeresearch: Techniques and procedures fordevelopinggrounded theory. Los Angeles: SAGE.*

Costa, N. C., & Alves, E. H. (1977). A semantical analysis of t he calculi \${bf C}_n\$. *Notre Dame Journal of Formal Logic, 18*(4), 621-630. doi:10.1305/ndjfl/1093888132

Russell, Gillian, "Logical Pluralism", THE STANFORD ENCYCLOPEDIA OF PHILOSOPHY (Spring 2019 Edition), Edward N. Zalta (ed.), URL = <https://plato.stanford.edu/archives/spr2019/entries/logical-pluralism/>.

Glaser, B. G., & Strauss, A. L. (1967). *The discovery of grounded theory: Strategies for qualitative research.*

Ferreira, L. B. (2012). Philosophy for Children in Science Class. Thinking: The Journalof Philosophy for Children,20(1), 73-81. doi:10.5840/thinking2012201/211

Hartshorne, R. (2000). *Geometry: Euclid and beyond.* New York: Springer.

Lakatos, I. (1962). *"Infinite Regress and Foundations of Mathematics",* ARISTOTELIAN SOCIETY SUPPLEMENTARY VOLUME, 36: 155–94.

Latour, B. (2002). We have never been modern. Cambridge, MA: Harvard University Press.

Mates, B. (1961). *Stoic logic.* Berkeley: University of California Press. Empírico, S., & Mates, B. (1996). *The Skeptic way: Sextus Empiricus "Outlines of Pyrrhonism".* New York: Oxford University Press.

Nightingale A (2013) Many roads from the axiom
of completeness. Questions Are Power,
    https://questionsarepower.files.wordpress.com/2016/03/ma
    ny_roads_from_the_axiom_of_compl etenes-2.pdf.

Nightingale, A. (2018). *Vagueness as the Embodiment of Inquiry:
An account of vagueness as it pertains to logic, and a study of
teaching vagueness to young Thai (P4) students.* Andrew
    Nightingale
https://questionsarepower.files.wordpress.com/2018/09/nighti
ngale- dissertation- vagueness-as-the-embodiment-of-inquiry.pdf

Peirce, C. S. (1933). *Collected Papers – IV Chapter 3 –
    Existential Graphs.*, pp. 4.397-4.417, edited by
    Charles Hartshorne and Paul Weiss, Harvard
    University Press, Cambridge.
Peirce, C. S., Hartshorne, C., Weiss, P., & Burks, A. W. (1960).
    Collected papers of Charles Sanders Peirce. (Vol 5).
    Cambridge: Belknap Press of Harvard University Press
Rowland, Tim. (2000). *The Pragmatics of Mathematics
    Education: Vagueness and Mathematical   Discourse
    (Studies in Mathematics Education Series, 14).* Taylor and
    Francis. Kindle Edition.
Russell, B.A.W. (1923). 'Vagueness', Australasian Journal of
    Psychology and Philosophy, 1, pp. 84–92.
Russell, B.A.W. (1923). *'Vagueness', Australasian Journal
    of Psychology and Philosophy*, 1, pp. 84– 92.
Russell, G., (2008), "One true logic?" JOURNAL OF
    PHILOSOPHICAL LOGIC, 37(6): 593–611.
Shapiro, S. (2008). *Vagueness in context.* Oxford
    University Press.
Tye, M. (1994). Sorites Paradoxes and the Semantics of
    Vagueness. *Philosophical Perspectives*,8, 189.
    doi:10.2307/2214170
Tarski, A. "On the Concept of Logical Consequence". In Logic,
    Semantics, Metamathematics: papers from 1923 to 1938,
    chapter 16, pages 409-420. Clarendon Press, Oxford,
    1956. Translated byJ. H. Woodger.

Vanier, L. (1884), *Jadis et Naguère*

Varzi, A. C., 2002, "On logical relativity,"
PHILOSOPHICAL ISSUES, 12: 197–219.

Weber, Z. (n.d.). Inconsistent Mathematics. Retrieved
from https://www.iep.utm.edu/math-inc/#H6

Wittgenstein, L., Bosanquet, R., & Diamond, C. (1976).
*Lectures on the foundations of mathematics: Cambridge,
1939*. Hassocks: Harvester

Wyatt, N., & Payette, G. (2019). Against logical generalism.
Synthese. doi:10.1007/s11229-018-02073- w

Many Roads from the Axiom of Completeness

Abstract

"We all grow up believing in the existence of real numbers . . ." (Abbot, 2001, p. 244). The "property that distinguishes" the real numbers is the Axiom of Completeness (Abbot, 2001, p. 244). The Axiom is a dry mathematical statement, or collection of equivalent statements. Jorge Luís Borges, the blind seer of metaphor (the dead root of every word), can help resurrect the dead metaphors behind the Axiom. It turns out the Axiom represents a wishful sort of thinking called logical induction. The desire behind induction is knowledge of the unknown, in the abstract. Does the Axiom give us knowledge of the unknown; does it solve ancient problems such as motion and being? Exploring what the Axiom means and what metaphors it hides releases a vertigo of ideas that swirl and coalesce into an inquiry into thinking of "the question" in itself. Imagining numbers without the grave Axiom leads one to wonder: Could an entirely different world of levity and wonder emerge?

Introduction

Jorge Luis Borges, in a lecture at Harvard, raised the possibility "that all metaphors are made by linking two different things together . . ." ("The Metaphor," 1967). His definition is circular because for any metaphor (as in "my heart is the sun") the "is" sets up a relation of equality ("heart" equals "sun"), making metaphor the relationship "is." What then "is" metaphor? In mathematics, "=" cannot stand with just one thing ("3 ="), even though "=" is often translated into English as "is."1 Borges says metaphor is circular by quoting the poet Lugones, a Spaniard who lived in Argentina the same time as Borges: "'Every word is a dead metaphor.' This of course is a metaphor" (Borges, 1967). Words are made of metaphors, and metaphors are made of words. Even the verb "to be" is a dead metaphor of something else. "To be" grew from the Proto-Indo-European "bheue" which also meant "to grow" and from "bheue" branched out into "bhumih"— "the world" in Sanskrit. One tries to speak simply of things being, but doing so links them to other things using dead metaphors. Borges offered the Chinese world of "the 10,000 things" and, by limiting himself to "metaphors that we feel *are* metaphors," he explored "stock" metaphors, which "appear in all literatures." Some metaphors repeat themselves over and over, which suggests a world of only "10,000 things" is possible. If one could only talk about things without the compounding effect of metaphors, would there be only 10,000 words, one for each thing, or would there be the well-explored labyrinth of infinity in mathematics?

Borges talks about one of the "stock" poetic metaphors: "We are such stuff. As dreams are made on" (Shakespeare, *The Tempest*, Act 4, Scene 1, 155–156). Here he notices a "slight contradiction" and asks, "If we are real in dreams, or if we are merely dreamers of dreams, then I wonder if we can make such sweeping statements." Mathematics does make "sweeping statements." In a world of metaphor, can these statements wake us up to the things themselves, things with a non-metaphorical being? Do we have the power to imagine our way out of the imagination, to perceive an awakening? Perhaps numbers have that power to take us through metaphor to the real things. Some consider the problem already settled, and one mathematician even said we are in an "era in which the real numbers are all-powerful" (Hartshorne, 2000, p. 3).

Before being sifted and refined into "real" ones, numbers are spoken, written and meant the same as words. The words "real numbers" mean that the numbers are real and not metaphorical, which entangles them in a complex relationship between Sign and Object. Why are they real and not metaphorical? How can anyone make the claim "numbers are real" without the implied metaphor of that statement?

The philosopher of science Paul Feyerabend argues that what a number is changed dramatically before Pythagoras's first revelation that "everything is number" and the painstaking work of proving the revelation that went on for millennia, almost to this day. "Examining archaic number concepts, many researchers assume that they share basic elements. Tables of addition, subtraction, multiplication, which are 'correct' when interpreted in modern terms, seem to confirm the assumption. But such an interpretation cannot explain why . . . the oldest known number systems were dyadic and why this feature survived right into the beginning of arithmetic" (Feyerabend, 1999, p. 88).

The story of how numbers made their progress toward reality is a myth that other fields share as well. Feyerabend continues by quoting Vasari, the first Italian art historian (see Vasari [1550, ed. 1568] cited in Feyerabend, 1999, pp. 89–90), who described how art progresses toward perfectly representing the real. Through stepping increments, saving the good from previous art and adding improvements, art reached perfection in Raphael of Urbino, whose "figures expressed perfectly the character of those they represented, the modest or the bold, being shown just as they are . . . , appear wholly realistic" (Feyerabend, 1999, pp. 89–90).

Mathematics proposes numbers to measure real things. There are notches corresponding to numbers on the measuring tape, but even if the notches succeed in referring to that real position. (although they remain a *sign* of the real object), gaps are still on the measuring tape with no notch and no number to describe the intermediate positions. The real number system attempts to fill the gaps that most numbers leave when describing something real, removing the need for metaphor. "Metaphorical language is language proper to the extent that it is related to the need for making up for gaps of language" (Giuliani, 1972, p. 131). The system "covers the gaps" and does the job of describing physical reality (and more) without metaphor. But how do real numbers go about covering the gaps?

Axiom of Completeness

The work of covering the gaps and freeing real numbers from metaphor is done with The Axiom of Completeness:

A bounded increasing sequence has a least upper bound (that is a real number)[2]

---

[2]"A bounded monotone sequence has a limit" is the definition given by Mattuck (1999, p. 11). I replace monotone with increasing and limit with least upper bound for clarity.

Why would the axiom of completeness cover all the gaps of a real line? A good example is in the act of measuring a plank with a straight-looking side. One compares the plank with a measuring tape and measures the whole meters, but there is still some plank left to measure. (The number of whole meters is the first number (position) in the sequence.) So one counts the number of decimeters left (the resulting position is the second number in the sequence), but there still remains more plank after the largest marker for decimeters. The process continues until the precision of the measuring tape is exhausted, eyesight fails, or the measurer loses interest. Even though one must fail in measuring the exact length of the plank, the axiom of completeness provides assurances that there exists a real number for the "actual" length of the plank (and that there is an "actual" length of the plank).

But the process cannot take the full measure of the plank, and so we remain in the poetic world of metaphor, "a process, not a definitive act; it is an inquiry, a thinking on" (Hejinian, 2000). We want to talk about something real, something as simple and straightforward as the length of a plank. We have an apparatus of controlled inquiry, tools and will-more than the casual use of words, but we still fail. We must admit that the measurements (words) we have used remain metaphorical and the actual measure of the plank (object) ultimately falls into the gaps of language. The words (measurements) we started with in our task of measuring the plank are no less metaphorical than the measurement we have when we stop. How can we wake up from metaphor?

The axiom of completeness assumes that the lingering question: "What is the next level of precision for measuring this plank?" is immaterial because we could answer each question by continuing the measurement process forever, if we set ourselves to the task (perhaps we could always pass the task on to our children). More importantly it seems to assume that our words lose their metaphorical quality in the limit of the sequence, asserting realism: Berkeley, who would not accept there were things no-one perceived, said realism was ". . . the absolute existence of unthinking things without any relation to their being perceived . . ." (quoted in Borges, 1964, p. 173).

The measurement example gets at the notion that real numbers are real and out there, and our method for finding them involves something like the scientific method. Charles Sanders Peirce, a philosopher traumatized with a rigorous mathematical education by his father, had this to say:

> It may be asked how I know that there are any Reals. If this hypothesis is the sole support of my method of inquiry, my method of inquiry must not be used to support my hypothesis. The reply is this: 1. If investigation cannot be regarded as proving that there are Real things, it at least does not lead to a contrary conclusion; but the method and the conception on which it is based remain ever in harmony. No doubts of the method, therefore, necessarily arise from its practice . . ." (Peirce, 1877/1992, p. 120)

The problem with Peirce's assertion is that there *are* doubts in any measurement of the plank. They take the form of questions. "Is that precise enough?" is a question that repeats at every measurement, and a measurement would not happen without the motivating question. What happens when the same doubt repeats over and over again? Often the question expands into other questions. "Why haven't I finished, am I doing something wrong?" To say no question of this kind *necessarily* arises is to put little faith in his students, as if they just do as their told.

The real number corresponding to the length of this plank is a least upper bound of a bounded (the plank is not infinite) sequence of measurements that is (the sequence) infinite and increasing. The measurement of the plank is an argument for the axiom of completeness, but it is incomplete because we cannot finish the measuring process, and we cannot speak about *all* such measurements (sequences mentioned in the Axiom). To more fully understand how the Axiom of Completeness creates the real numbers, and to discover the "escape" from metaphor, requires understanding how the Axiom is a "sweeping statement" (Borges, 1967).

Induction

A generalization such as "All crows are black," made before we have complete knowledge of all crows, is the archetypal "sweeping statement." That move, called induction, leaps from the known— shaky as it is—to an unknown. The (often wrong) assumption is that the unknown will be similar in some way to the known. The *Oxford English Dictionary* says induction is a logical movement from the specific to the general. In math, however, induction can go from the specific to the more specific. For example, take the decimal number derived from measuring. The numbers written down are not as specific as the finished decimal expansion, the real number, of the "actual" measure. The real number (represented with ". . ." for "the rest" because it cannot be fully written or expressed) refers to the findings of an infinite investigation. One cannot know the results and so uses induction to infer what the results might be.

In induction, confusion arises between the potential and the actual. Are we saying that the results might be or that they are? Aristotle mentions this confusion: ". . . to a never-ending process of division, we attribute an actuality which exists potentially." And this confusion is not surprising, because induction represents what we wish logic could do; what deduction cannot do.

Hume, the 18th century Scottish philosopher noticed what induction was based on: "that instances of which we have had no experience, must resemble those of which we have had experience, and that the course of nature continues always uniformly the same" (1888, p. 89). Concerning that uniformity he argues, "The principle cannot be proved deductively" (Vickers, 2012, p. 7). Any regularity in observed things could imply order or chaos in unobserved things, and neither is necessary deductively. Using induction would require we already knew the order of nature, which is circular.

Hume reasoned that induction is not the work of reason, and so it must be the result of the imagination. "The force of induction, the force that drives the inference is thus not an objective feature of the world, but a subjective power, the mind's capacity to form inductive habits . . . inductive inference, is thus an illusion, an instance of what Hume calls the minds "great propensity to spread itself on external objects" (Hume, 1888, p. 167, cited in Vickers, 2012, p. 8).

Some texts do offer a proof of the axiom of completeness (Abbott, 2001, p. 245), but still use induction, and "induction brings with it the risk of error" (Vickers, 2012, p. 5). [3]

Error can be found in the assumption that the unknown will resemble the known. But none of the possible error has a space in the "gapless" real number line. At each stage in the plank example, the measurement takes the form of action to find an answer that takes one back to a question—a dialogue between word and object, or between person and object. A dialectic model, raised before the real numbers arrive, does have room for the inductive error, as well as room for questions.

---

[3]Dedekind "cuts," defined as real numbers, are sets that can be characterized by a bounded, infinite and increasing sequence, just like the Axiom of Completeness. The difference is in name only. The infinite process is called an (open) set, and the set is then called a real number

There is some history and difference of opinion on what induction is. Peirce says induction is something else, a logical move where the result is *different* from the premises (Peirce, "The Probability of Induction," 1878/1992, p. 162), anticipating Borges: ". . . the metaphor is a linking of two different things together . . ." (1967, Lecture, "The Metaphor"). The leap from metaphor to induction does not seem so wide under these definitions. But there is a difference. The real numbers emerged from many inductions, asserting a "natural" order to space and time. The belief in that nature shakes the sleeper awake, but the metaphor connecting waking life and the dream vanishes. The metaphor is replaced with induction, an unending task of refining words (measurements) toward actualizing the real numbers.

". . . that the rule of induction will hold good in the long run may be deduced from the principle that reality is only the object of the final opinion to which sufficient investigation would lead" (Peirce 1878, p. 169). When have we investigated the plank sufficiently? What about the rest of the plank? Where do we rest after the investigation, on the questions that result or on the final measurement? Peirce says in an earlier essay (1877) that uncertainty can only give dissatisfaction, and because of this "Reals" such as the "actual" measure of the plank cannot be doubted. Here he is ignoring skepticism, which practices a peaceful state in accepting a lack of certainty (see Pyrrhonism, in Suber, 1996).

The measurement of the plank is, metaphorically speaking, the progression of human knowledge and the movement from word to object. The axiom of completeness is the completion of this progression, this movement. We can begin to see why the Axiom is so useful. Once assumed as a premise, deduction₄ (like the usual Aristotelian logic) empowers us to demonstrate the synthetic quality of our knowledge, to find "new" knowledge. But, Peirce says,". . . a synthetic inference cannot by any means be reduced to deduction . . ." (1878/1992, p. 162). Unfortunately his saying so cannot stop authors of scientific papers and teachers of mathematics, by assuming the Axiom of Completeness, from doing it anyway.

It seems we can imagine an awakening with the axiom of completeness. What is this awakening like? What is this new knowledge we have assumed?

Wakefulness

In our example of measuring the plank we make a leap of logic to say something about *all* future measurements called induction. There is also an induction on all these inductions in the axiom of completeness, which talks not just about *this* plank and *this* induction on a sequence of measurements but about *all* of the similar types of measurements. The axiom of completeness ends up being the Induction of induction within the language of the real numbers. Just as the "King of kings" is another word for God, the Axiom of Completeness has ultimate say-so over the "real" world; every point in space is perfectly ordered and defined, it is imagined, well beyond the slightest detectible degree. An idealist would admit there is an infinite intelligence keeping an awareness of our ordered world everywhere we have not, or cannot look.

₄Deduction (like the usual Aristotelian logic) is not induction, it cannot tell anyone what they don't know based on what they know. It will only tell them what they already know in different ways.

Mathematics is not alone in turning to God for answers on the non-metaphorical whatness of things. Aristotle, on the question "What is being?" said a composite thing was something in addition to its parts: ". . . this additional something is not an element but . . . the cause," and Aristotle's First Mover causes everything (*Metaphysics*, 1980, pp. 135–36).

The justification for the Axiom of Completeness is that without it numbers fail, just as words do, in describing the world. Successfully assuming the Axiom comes with a cost. The Axiom takes the students of real numbers down a path that has no possibilities, no holes or gaps where their decisions are important. Bugaev, a father figure in the rise of the mathematical school of Moscow, argued against the focus on completeness, saying incompleteness (or discontinuity) is a ". . . manifestation of independent individuality and autonomy" (Bugaev, 1897, quoted in Graham and Kantor, 2009, p. 68).

For all the deductive thinking that follows in a math textbook on real numbers (Abbott, 2001, Mattuck, 1999), it may be said that *thought itself has been excluded.* Any time that readers confront a situation of considering something, where they "really" may go one way or another with their thoughts, the book asserts necessity, and students don't have much choice but to follow along. The lingering questions are controlled: "What is the next level of precision?" and then all are answered, but only by saying the unfinished sequence of measurements "is finished" — the *number* —"is real."

This world of perfect wakefulness is also static. Zeno of Elea, a pre-Socratic philosopher and follower of Parmenides, believed all was one and thus change must be an illusion. Zeno argued that motion is not possible under the model of the real number line. One of his objections is illustrated in the story of Achilles and the Tortoise. The Tortoise is given a head start in his racing match against the demi-god. After the Tortoise runs a distance, Achilles begins running, and quickly runs the same distance. The tortoise has moved since Achilles started running, however, and is still ahead of Achilles by a shorter distance. Achilles runs this shorter distance in a small amount of time, but the Tortoise again has used the small amount of time to get ahead of Achilles. The result is an infinite sequence where the tortoise is always ahead of Achilles, and Achilles cannot win the race without completing an infinite task. Any motion of any speed, simply by hypothesizing a similar race, will require an infinite task to complete. The same argument can be used, not to prove motion is impossible, but that motion is *not expressible with points*. The problem Zeno put forth, the problem of completing an infinite task, is not dealt with in real number or calculus texts (Abbott, 2001), but is covered up under the name "limit." Having a name for an infinite task does not make it any less infinite. Aristotle writes that "every motion is incomplete" (*Metaphysics*, 1980, p. 152). In this perfect wakefulness, the light does not radiate, does not twinkle, no-one blinks.

The divine project of the language of real numbers, completed by the axiom, is reminiscent of the story of the Tower of Babel.

> In a mixture of positivism and myth, Dante attributes the rise of different languages to the occupational diversity required for building the Tower of Babel. The members of each trade or profession had their own language . . . . And perhaps with theological Latin in mind, he says that the higher the intellectual quality of the specialty, the more barbarous the language. (Burke, 1950, p. 168)

Real numbers can't be written or spoken since their expression is infinite. On the language of the underworld in the Book of Thoth, "difficult are their words; their repetitions (or explanations) being too various to write . . ." (Jasnow, Lewis, and Zauzich, 2005, p. 63). We have conceived of an unspeakable language. In the silence, what has happened to poetry? The "thinking on" is over, now that we know everything. And poetry is when ". . . felt I like the watcher of skies / When a new planet swims into his ken" (Keats, 1816/1870).

The price of perfect wakefulness is paid by surrendering motion, and among the losses associated with that loss is the loss of discovery in poetry, and perhaps even life if Borges is right in saying, ". . . life is, I am sure, made of poetry" (Lecture, 1967). Imposing the Axiom of Completeness is not malicious, but springs from an intense desire to know. All is in motion, even things at rest move through time; *complete* certainty requires the end of motion. The Axiom stands for that surrender, that utter pessimism that knowing is better than being open to possibility. But the loss of motion is not well represented to math students, whose teachers instead claim that now they can fully describe— that is, *know*— motions with continuous functions (Abbott, 2001).

Motion

Continuity has the connotation of movement. The real number line is continuous by the axiom of completeness. What is continuity? It is like "smoothness," but no one possesses a fine enough magnifying glass to ensure that a line remains uniform or telescope to ensure it remains smooth forever, and so we use induction to infer smoothness. Continuity of a line requires completeness or "gaplessness."

The "stock" metaphor for continuity of time is a river flowing (Borges, 1967). The prime quality of water is that no matter how you magnify, that is, divide out a smaller portion of it), the water remains the same. It is akin to saying water has no qualities, and closer inspection reveals the featurelessness of water. For the most part, water only takes on the features of its container. Although Heraclitus said, "you cannot go into the same water twice" (quoted by Plato, "The Cratylus," 1892, p. 92), the second time in, the water has all the same features as the water the first time. Heraclitus also said, "We step and do not step in the same rivers, we are and are not" (Russell, 1918, p. 16). Continuity in math is like the experience of flowing water, and is also described intuitively as drawing the graph of a function without taking your pencil off the paper; the motion continues without sudden change or leap across a gap.

Newton asserted in his first law of motion: "Every body left to itself moves uniformly in a straight line" (quoted in Heidegger, 1977, p. 262). Zeno's objections aside, the real number line represents Newton's theory of motion best. The natural state of motion is a "uniform" or continuous one, and in a single direction. Heidegger writes that Newton begins in his first axiom of motion with "corpus omne," "every body," which means that the Aristotelian distinction between earthly and celestial bodies "has become obsolete" (Heidegger, 1977, p. 262). Aristotle asserted the existence of two "natural" motions of these two bodies: gravity and levity. Gravity moves in a straight line down, and levity moves up and eventually in circles in the heavens. But after Newton, the two natural motions no longer exist. Instead motion has only one nature—continuity or "uniformity" in a straight line, and one body described with real numbers.

The straight line requires opposition between positive and negative, or any other coupling of opposites. The spectrum of possible scores on the SAT, for example, places people along a line with two extremes and describes them with real numbers, and then uses the scores, monstrously, to decide in part a student's future. The "bodies" that live between any two opposites are of one type, described as real numbers. Their natural motion is of one type, in gradations that proceed continuously in a straight line. Time itself is no longer a "garden of forking paths" (Borges, 1941/1964), winding and separating, but one straight super highway to an infinite horizon. Escaping from the dream of metaphor involves following this highway, but succeeding the escape comes at the cost of accepting the Axiom.

The model of the straight line between opposites was not always universal. Heidegger offers that this model replaces any "agon" between opposites, where agon means strife or competition. Celestial motion was circular, which Aristotle argues cannot be defined in terms of an opposition (Aristotle, *Physics*, 1980, p. 176). One concept (such as the present you, reading) and the idea of constantly returning to the present you, reading, is enough for circular motion. What motivation could there be for Newton, a devout Christian with a famous saintly persona, to minister the world out of the heavenly movements, into a world characterized by competition of opposites, and survival of the fittest?

In our example of measuring the plank, the dialectic process is what some call the essence of motion. Apart from Newton, Marx believed the human world would eventually be characterized by free association and cooperation (Marx, 1875). Lenin reported that Marx believed dialectics is "the science of the general laws of motion both of the external world and of human thought" (Lenin, 1980). Teachers of analysis encourage thinking through a proof of continuity with the dialectic relationship between two shrinking quantities called epsilon and delta. This is because epsilon is a response to an arbitrary choice of the value (or dialectical position) of delta. After thinking it through dialectically the student removes the dialectic "shape" and replaces it with a logical proof.

The quantities *epsilon* and *delta* are "open sets." The definition of a real open set "G" requires a notion of a "neighborhood" around every point "a" in "G" that is complete like the real numbers. Such a positive definition of an open set is possible because of the Axiom of Completeness, because the neighborhood is complete. Without the axiom of completeness, open sets would have to be *dialectically* defined. "[T]he dialectical definition does not aim in short at determining the essence, but the limits of a proposed definition" (Guilani, 1972, p. 131). Open sets are simply not their boundaries. When you say "not the boundary (or limit)" you indirectly get the same completeness of an open set, but without a positive definition. Some boundaries would require on-going inquiry to find. Dialectically defined open sets make for a different kind of mathematics of continuity, difficult in different ways, but the basic idea of an open set is easier to state and oppose to "closed sets" (the opposite of an open set, defined as a set that contains all its "boundaries" or limit points).

Continuity (and movement) need not be a result of the Axiom of Completeness, because a dialectic process can describe continuity instead (incompletely, vaguely). The axiom of completeness removes the need for dialectically defined objects, as well as metaphor, within the language of the real numbers. Life goes on, but after the acceptance of the Axiom life has changed. Followers of the Axiom have no place in time or space. "In time, because if the future and the past are infinite, there will not really be a when; in space, because if every being is equidistant from the infinite and the infinitesimal, there will not be a where. No one exists on a certain day, in a certain place; no one knows the size of his face." (Borges, 1964, p. 8)

The wakefulness we find from the Axiom seems to falter, and thinking about what should be done continues. Questions motivate and connect the various positions in dialectical process. Without questions there can be no internal motion, but Aristotle would extend this to the external world by saying motion cannot exist without potential. Questions are an expression of many potential answers, many possible paths. Do we follow this image of the real line, a single super highway to the horizon, or do we wonder which path takes us there?

Questions

Aristotle believes levity is a natural motion upwards possessed by only certain kinds of bodies. Today Newton's laws of motion include gravity but not levity and only one kind of body, all under the pull of gravity. Questions, at least internally, offer a necessary form of thought, different from answers such as real numbers, a form of thought that expands, and leads to an uplifting sense of wonderment. Levity has not left us internally, but what about externally? Is levity real, with all the "weight" that reality must have?

What are questions? For an example of the question itself, "This is a question" doesn't work because it is not a question. Referring to the question with a question: "Is this a question?" seems to be an example of the question itself. Is it a question whether we ask it or not, the way answers are discovered? If the answer is no, then "Is this a question?" isn't always a question. That is, if we write it down in a book and forget about it, that it is a question ceases to be true. As soon as we stop asking it, it would have to disappear. If I confirm "Is this a question" is a question over and over again, using induction is appropriate to say that "Is this a question?" is, internally, a real question. But, the use of induction here brings us to a paradox- as soon as we use induction to conclude that "Is this a question?" IS a question, "Is this a question?" is not in question. After all, how could this question be, if its being were not in question? We cannot even say that "Is this a question?" is real *internally*, but there is still the problem that every time I ask, and before I answer, "Is this a question?" it seems to be a question. So we rest, for now, on the conclusion that the question is, internally, not unreal. We are limited on both sides, inconclusively, the inductive conclusion that the question is real cannot be made, yet the question itself is confirmable in a way that makes it seem real.

Questions are elusive and hard to pin down as objects of thought, yet they are indispensable for dialectical process. Thought itself moves naturally between certainty and inquiry. We use questions every day, and looking for a definition of the question justifies the dialectical definition in general; even though it is imprecise it is the best we can do. It is expected that questions will not be easily discovered externally, as potential, but will naturally avoid definition. Questioning is a necessary part of dialectical movement, therefore questions are a necessary part of thought. If thought has any physical reality (perhaps in the brain), then so does questioning have a physical reality. It has been shown that it is not so simple to claim that the question is "real." Perhaps exploring the question as an expression of potential can help.

A rock on the top of a hill has potential energy. The potential to move a long way by rolling down the hill, but where, on what plane, is this potential perceivable? The rock has potential because it has not rolled down the hill. An empty vessel has the potential to be filled, as does a gap in language. Metaphor fills gaps by linking the gap to other words. The link is like a part of a web. Because of our difficulty with defining the question itself, it is understandable to be wary of settling on the idea that potential is "not-being" or a hole or gap. The problem of defining power is more difficult than "not-being"; the lack of a person in front of me does not mean there is the potential for one to appear magically before me. The web is an apt metaphor for power- it must have holes to be, but not everything is possible because the web has a structure in its links. Foucault argued the model for power was a web, but well before that the Greek myth of Arachne made it clear the webs humans weave have the power to rival the gods. In the Book of Thoth it is written, "What is the taste of the prescription of writing? What is this net?" (Jasnow, Lewis, and Zauzich, 2005, p. 16)

Numbers *before* the Axiom of Completeness are arranged in a web, like the grid on graph paper, but the web of lines on the graph paper is Euclidean, and that is a particular kind of web with parallel lines that are straight and equidistant. The Euclidean web makes distance measurable with numbers. There are other kinds of webs. A web with curved links is not measurable unless it is translatable into a Euclidean web.[5]

---

[5]Unless we grossly redefine distance, and in these cases there are multiple viable definitions for distance. I do not use "translate" in a technical sense.

A common argument for real numbers filling the gaps of a line is to draw a square with a side equal to one unit and then draw the diagonal inside the square. The diagonal, by the Pythagorean theorem, has a length of the square-root of two, which turns out to be a hole in the smaller number systems before the real numbers. The argument is to show someone a length with no number to emphasize the need for a better number system. Such an argument depends on Euclidean space, however, and depends on the perfectly straight lines found in Euclidean space. The epic history of mathematicians trying to prove Euclidean geometry as the one true geometry has never ended in success (Hartshorne, 2000, p. 304). Instead, other geometries have been admitted for study, but where does that leave our argument for the existence of the square-root of two? The construction of the square and its diagonal is just one possibility, one rhetorical posture. Possibilities for rhetorical argument *against* the existence of real numbers are also available using different "webs."

Thinking in a language with *no* gaps such as the real numbers, is thought with *no* potential. The real numbers do not make a web; they are "completely" connected. The real numbers create a "real" world of orderly and knowable space and time, and in doing so it has a power to completely describe this "real" world, so that real numbers seem to be "all powerful" (Hartshorne, 2000, p. 3). The perfectly known world lacks potential "completely," however. Numbers are powerful, but the rhetorical choice of words such as "real numbers" (potential numbers?) and "completeness" is a treatment of infinity as an actuality, and make it clear that the power of numbers is not to be given to math students. The secret to the real numbers is there *is* a hole- and that hole is the lack of potential, of "The Question."

Questions are not unreal. They are not included in Newton's statement about "every body," since they cannot be represented with real numbers (which are answers). Mathematicians attempt to know "real" numbers even though there are more of them than can be literally expressed. Questions are capable of suggesting more than they are capable of literally expressing- they suggest many answers at once, in a more simple way than real numbers do. Taking the inductive leap to say questions are real only arrives at a paradox. We cannot say questions, in general, are real. Is the paradox a contradiction? Is "Is this a question?" a material counter-example against induction? The spaces that these questions inhabit are not to be found on the real line; numbers cannot answer them.

Conclusion

> Concerning the basic law of motion, the law of inertia, the question arises whether this law is not to be subordinated under a more general one, i.e., the law of conservation of energy, which is now determined according to its expenditure and consumption, as work, . . . questionability is concealed by the results and the progress of scientific work." (Heidegger, 1977, p. 270)

Statistics, physics, and economics do work that depends on the Axiom of Completeness, as does any topic that uses continuous functions. High school mathematics textbooks assume the axiom of completeness implicitly, and the Axiom enters explicit study up to the graduate level. The work that college math students of the Axiom then do tends to proceed deductively, and so can be clear only internally (the internal logic is clearly necessary), but the meaning of their work—the external synthesis with the world- their Metaphor—is not explored.

It is certain that such a synthesis is of epic proportion, but with only deductions, the mathematics amounts to externally mysterious re-phrasings of the Axiom. Math textbooks (e.g., Mattuck, 1999) use extremely short summaries of the deep philosophical and rhetorical problems of the Axiom and offer them as assumptions (Abbott, 2001), then conceal the questionability of the assumptions by directing students to work at solving problems and deducing theorems. Having students accept what the textbooks say without discussion, controversy and reading into the deep problems of completeness, continuity, and motion is the opposite of education.

Aristotle would object that there are no holes or gaps found anywhere (Aristotle, *Physics*, 1980), and perhaps in space, motion cannot be in a vacuum, but the old theory of ether resurfaces to explain movement: "the ether hypothesis was bound always to play some part in physical science, even if at first only a latent part" (Einstein, 1922). And this latent part it plays is as a medium. "Newtonian . . . [gravity] . . . is only apparently immediate action at a distance, but in truth is conveyed by a medium permeating space, whether by movements or by elastic deformation of this medium." (Einstein, 1922). If so this medium could not be thought of as abundant in spaces and rare in particles, which would require another medium between these particles. Instead the metaphor for "ether" could be as a "cloud," and not the way a cloud in the sky is thought of today which is as particles and space. Instead, if one must think in particles/points, it may be thought that the particles are in more than one place, or in indefinite spaces at once.

Unlike the Axiom of Completeness, which asserts every position is knowable, these "clouds" are vague notions representing potential instead of certainty; they are bodies of levity. They are not unreal, but they are not exactly there; they are here as well.

The proof that the square root of two is not a rational number (and therefore is one of the holes the Axiom fills with real numbers) is essentially a poem, grasping at the inexpressible and failing. The square-root of 2 is indefinite, and the statement, "The square-root of 2 is a quantity," are spoken metaphorically.

"The Question" overarches and connects difficult questions in philosophy, such as the role of potential in the hard problem of motion, what is knowable, or whether humans are dreams or real. The axiom of completeness defines the numbers we use to describe ourselves, our futures (GPAs, exam scores). The Axiom seems to be "The Answer" in a state of opposition to "The Question." The Axiom is so extreme that arguing against it is polarizing. The reality is that there is not one path away from the Axiom. Any thought or decision multiplies these forking paths, making us wonder more and more. Motion and its dialogue continue. "Have I dreamt my life or was it a true one?" The German poet Vogelweide asked in his poem, "Ah! Where are the hours departed fled!" (c. 1200). Comparing Vogelweide's line to Shakespeare's "We are such stuff as dreams are made on," Borges offers, "instead of a sweeping affirmation, we have a question . . . and this hesitation gives us that dreamlike essence" (Borges, "The Metaphor," 1967).

Ah! where are hours departed fled?

Is life a dream, or true indeed?

Did all my heart hath fashioned From

fancy's visitings proceed?

Yes! I have slept; and now unknown

To me the things best known before:

The land, the people, once mine own,

Where are they? — they are here no more . . .

Works Cited

Abbott, Stephen. *Understanding Analysis*. New York: Springer, 2001.

Aristotle. *The Physics*. Translated by H. G. Apostle. Grinnell, Iowa: Peripatetic Press, 1980.

Aristotle. *The Metaphysics*. Translated by H. G. Apostle. Grinnell, Iowa: Peripatetic Press, 1980.

Berkeley, George, and Howard Robinson. *Principles of Human Knowledge and, Three Dialogues*. Oxford: Oxford University Press, 1999.

Borges, Jorge Luís. "The Metaphor." *The Riddle of Poetry*. Lectures delivered in Cambridge, MA, Fall 1967. http://www.youtube.com/watch?v=vL_86Ckp1E0.

Borges, Jorge Luís. *Other Inquisitions, 1937–1952*. Austin: University of Texas Press, 1964.

Bugaev, Nicolai. "Les mathematiques et la conception du monde au point de vue de la phuosophie scientifique." Address, Proceedings of the International Congress of Mathematicians from International Congress of Mathematicians, Zurich, August 9, 1897.

Burke, Kenneth. *Rhetoric of Motives*. Berkeley: University of California Press, and New York: Prentice-Hall, 1950.

Einstein, Albert. *Ether and the Theory of Relativity*. Methuen & Co. Ltd, London, 1922.

Feyerabend, Paul. *Conquest of Abundance: A Tale of Abstraction Verses the Richness of Being*. Chicago: University of Chicago Press, 1999.

Giuliani, Alessandro. "The Aristotelian Theory of Dialectical Definition." *Philosophy & Rhetoric* 5, no. 3 (Summer 1972): 129– 142.

Graham, Loren R., and Jean Kantor. *Naming infinity a true story religious mysticism and mathematical creativity.* Cambridge, Mass.: Belknap Press of Harvard University Press, 2009.

Hartshorne, Robin. *Geometry: Euclid and Beyond.* New York: Springer, 2000.

Heidegger, Martin. *Basic Writings: From Being and Time (1927) to The Task of Thinking (1964).* New York: Harper & Row, 1977.

Hejinian, Lyn. "The Language of Inquiry." Poets.org. http://www.poets.org/viewmedia.php/prmMID/16195#sthash.Tin ABY7K.dpuf (accessed May 12, 2014).

Hume, David. *Treatise of Human Nature.* 1739–1740. Ed. L. A. Selby Bigge. Oxford: Clarendon Press, 1888.

Jasnow, Richard Lewis, and Karl Zauzich. *The ancient Egyptian Book of Thoth: A demotic discourse on knowledge and pendant to the classical hermetica.* Wiesbaden: Harrassowitz Verlag, 2005.

Jowett, Benjamin. *Cratylus.* Champaign, Ill.: Project Gutenberg, 1990.

Keats, John. "On First Looking into Chapman's Homer." 1817. Poetry Foundation. http://www.poetryfoundation.org/poem/173746 (accessed May 12, 2014).

Lenin, Vladimir Ilyich. *On the question of dialectics: A collection.* Moscow: Progress, 1980.

Lugones, Leopoldo, and Jesus Benítez. *Lunario sentimental.* Madrid: Catedra, 1988.

Marx, Karl. "Critique of the Gotha Programme—III." http://www.marxists.org/archive/marx/works/1875/gotha/ch03.ht m (accessed May 12, 2014).

Mattuck, Arthur. *Introduction to analysis.* Upper Saddle River, N.J.: Prentice Hall, 1999.

Peirce, C. S. *The Essential Peirce: Selected Philosophical Writings Vol. 1.* Ed. Nathan Houser, Christian Kloesel, Nathan Houser, and Christian Kloesel. Bloomington: Indiana University Press, 1992.

Plato. *The Dialogues, Vol. 2*, 3d ed. Translated by Benjamin Jowett. Oxford, 1892, www.gutenberg.org.

Russell, Bertrand. *Mysticism and Logic and other essays.* Nottingham: Spokesman, 2007.

Shakespeare, William. *The Tempest By Mr. William Shakespear.* London: Printed for J. Tonson, and the rest of the proprietors; and sold by the Booksellers of London and Westminster, 1734.

Suber, Peter. "Classical Skepticism." 1996 http://legacy.earlham.edu/~peters/writing/skept.htm (accessed May 12, 2014).

Vickers, John. "The Problem of Induction." Stanford University. http://plato.stanford.edu/archives/spr2013/entries/induction-problem. (accessed May 12, 2014).

Vogelweide, Walther von der. "Poetry." *Ah! Where Are Hours Departed Fled?* (excerpt) by Walther von der Vogelweide. http://www.oldpoetry.com/Walther_von_der_Vogelweide/853829 9-Ah_Where_Are_Hours_Departed_Fled_excerpt (accessed May 12, 2014).

Whitehead, Alfred North, and Bertrand Russell. *Principia mathematica*, 2d ed. Cambridge: Cambridge University Press, 1925–1927.

Vagueness as the Embodiment of Inquiry: An account of Vagueness as it pertains to logic and a study of teaching vagueness to young Thai (P4) students

Abstract

The goal of this project was to make visible to students the instability of classical logic and probability theory, which in turn makes the instability of the foundations of other sciences visible. After a philosophical contribution on the nature and ramifications of vagueness (as the embodiment of inquiry), innovative act-ivies that were invented for the students to encounter vagueness and logical pluralism are presented. Finally, the methodology of action research and grounded theory was employed for the empirical part of this thesis. How would students respond to learning about these instabilities, which ultimately stem from the problem of vagueness? It was found that vagueness is a very difficult topic to learn about. However students did not shy away from investigating vagueness, who, especially students previously deemed "bad," engaged in intense sensory investigation. The students mentioned that this kind of investigation was not common in their science classes. A significant finding was that students are more interested in vague situations than non-vague situations.

KEY WORDS: VAGUENESS / LOGICAL PLURALISM / MATHEMATICS EDUCATION / PHILOSOPHY FOR CHILDREN (P4C)

Introduction

Today, some high school students study logic, many recognize a truth table immediately, while others have had no logic training. Most students, especially non-physical science majors, tend not to study logic in college. Colleges of the past taught geometry as absolutely true, but now it is a place to encounter non-Euclidean geometry. Entering college students find a multiplicity of cultures, disciplines and ideas. The different students and teachers who have moved away from family and neighborhood converge at the university: a place where variety of ideas are the mainstay. Multiplicity is important to education— the sensitivity towards many differences is a sign of a good education and a keen mind. The treatment of logic looks monotheistic in this context. While there is usually an offered course in logic it only shows one kind of the various logics being applied in science today. Usually there is no recognition that probability theory is another kind of fuzzy logic, seeming to add to the narrative that there is only one logic.

> "The whole essence of Russell's view [in Principia Mathematica] is that there is only one logic. There must not be a Russellian and a non-Russellian logic, in the way in which there is a Euclidean and a non-Euclidean geometry." (Wittgenstein 1976, p172)

Why is there no logic course offering multiple logics in the university? Perhaps it is because the need for multiple logics is not well perceived. Logical pluralism has received new scholarly interest culminating in Beall and Restall's (2006) book on logical pluralism. They say that the reason or motivation for logical pluralism is that logic (specifically logical consequence or the if, then) is vague. The bond between vagueness and logic is a strong one and written about extensively. Ultimately this is a dissertation about the bond between vagueness and logic, with the proposal that the bond between them is found in the activity of inquiry. Dewey (1938) proposed that logic is the result of inquiry. Here I propose that vagueness is also the result of inquiry, a real result. Vagueness is the experiential body of logical inquiry, or inquiry into logic. It is because vagueness arises in inquiry (and therefore logic) that logical pluralism is favored.

1.1 Some history of logical pluralism

The Stoics bring us several formulations of logical consequence (Mates, 1961). There were at least four types of logical consequence that were proposed during the Stoic debates. In the Philonian view, a statement of logical consequence was true except when the antecedent was true and the consequent false (This is the truth table kind taught in logic classes today). The Diodorean view is stronger, saying that it must be impossible at any time for the antecedent to be true and the consequent false. An even stronger logical consequence was one that was only true when the negation of the consequent is incompatible with its antecedent. "If Atomic elements do not exist, then atomic elements do exist" is true in the previous two senses, but false in this third sense. Finally, a conditional is true when the consequent is contained in the antecedent. "If it is day, then it is day," is true in the previous three cases but false in this fourth case, since "it is day" is not strictly contained by "it is day."

However Stoics were interested in picking one of these, the plurality of logic was only allowed because different individuals such as Philo and Diodorus conversed. Logical pluralism of today, on the other hand, may have a kind of dialectical existence, but the pluralism can be upheld by one person.

After Aristotle's contribution to logic, philosophers in the west for thousands of years up to and including Kant, believed logic was fully discovered. It wasn't until non-Euclidean geometry was discovered that doubt was cast on other previously certain knowledge. Logical pluralism is, from an historical point of view, a revolutionary topic. Euclid's geometry books taught geometry in a landmark form: the axiomatic form. From simple assumptions (axioms) Euclid built theorems that were proven using classical logic and some arithmetic-like postulates.

> "Lakatos showed in this paper [1962] how one of the traditional ways of attempting to justify some branch of knowledge has been to try to find some indubitably true 'first principles', containing only 'crystal clear' terms, from which the whole of that branch of knowledge is derivable via the infallibly truth preserving rules of deductive logic. Any such attempt Lakatos called 'Euclidean'..." (Worrall 1976, p 3)

Logical pluralism is a very different perspective from having one "infallible" deductive logic. It begins by showing why one logic is problematic, and leads to other possible ways to justify knowledge. First of all, there are no 'crystal clear' terms, "All language is vague" (Russell 1923, p 1). The form of teaching logical pluralism may well prove as fundamental as the 'Euclidean' form.

An old kind of logical pluralism by Carnap is that different languages give rise to different logics. "According to Carnap... to be tolerant about language choice is already to be tolerant about choice of logic—for languages so-conceived come with different logics already 'built in.' "(Russell 2013)

1.2 Current situation

These considerations gain importance when current scholars of logic assert "Logical consequence [the if, then] is the central concept in logic. The aim of logic is to clarify what follows from what. - Stephen Read, Thinking about Logic [99]" (As quoted in Beall, Restall 2006, Kindle Location 192) According to Tarski, logical consequence can be clarified in more than one way, giving rise to more than one equally valid (if applied in different situations) formulation of logical consequence. "Any attempt to bring into harmony all possible vague, sometimes contradictory, tendencies which are connected with the use of this concept[logical consequence], is certainly doomed to failure. We must reconcile ourselves to the fact that every precise definition of [logical consequence] will show arbitrary features to a greater or less degree." (Tarski "On the Concept of Logical Consequence" reprinted 1956, p 409 as quoted by Beall and Restall 2006, Kindle Locations 115-117, my emphasis) The solution to the vagueness of logical consequence, rather, lies in logical pluralism. And a logical pluralism within the same language. "(Restall 2000; Paoli 2003)... if the meanings of the logical expressions are governed by...rules ...two logics can agree on those rules, whilst disagreeing on the relation of logical consequence. Hence even if you have successfully chosen a language, it seems that you might not yet have determined a logic. " (Russell 2013)

The vagueness of logical consequence effects, or is effected by, all language—so that in a given case where logical consequence is applied, it is vague what the conclusion could be, allowing conflicting results. And there are examples of such instances—instances where constructive logic, paraconsistent logic and classical logic, all in the same language, disagree on conclusions.

The point is if I get contradictory reports, then whether you think me rational or irrational depends upon what I do with the reports. If I react by saying, "Well, there are 30,000 and there are 40,000", you would say "What on earth do you mean?" you might say, "Surely you can't imagine there being 30,000 and 40,000." But this could be answered in all sorts of ways. I might even draw picture of it—for instance a blurred picture..." (Wittgenstein 1939, p201)

The vague landscape can become more clear by turning to Dewey's theory of logic. Dewey believed that logic formed from inquiry, that is, from empirical investigation, and became the form of further inquiry. "the view here expressed, they (logical laws) represent conditions which have been ascertained during the conduct of continued inquiry to be involved in its own successful pursuit." (Dewey 1938 Loc 284-286). Logic arises from inquiry, and since the senses cannot give a fully clear picture, logics, as sources of clarity, conflict. Vagueness, it will be argued, as a kind of physical indeterminacy, is the embodiment of inquiry, of the uncertainty that fuels inquiry. That is the present thesis, and it is in a way opposite to Dewey's thesis in "Logic as Inquiry" because logic is viewed (and viewed by Dewey) as an enterprise fundamentally against vagueness (Russell 1923), an enterprise of "precision knowledge." However in a way this thesis is complementary to Dewey's view. Logic is inquiry and vagueness is inquiry, since both are results of empirical investigation. Some of Dewey's work stands in support of the general thesis presented here. Precision should not be pursued for its own sake.

"The modern theory, derived, as has been said, from the attempt to retain forms after their material or existential content had been abandoned, is grounded in nothing and leads nowhere. It is formal only in the sense of being empty and mechanical. It neither reflects existence already known nor forwards inquiry into what may and should be known. It is a logical vermiform appendix. (Dewey 1938, Loc 3391-3397)

Under Dewey's pragmatism, Channell investigates vagueness and finds "Vague language forms a considerable part of language use. The corpora and other texts studied show many examples, occurring in a wide range of contexts. This means we cannot, in any theory of language, treat it as the exception rather than the rule." (Channell 1994, p 198)

Vagueness has been formulated and studied since the ancient Greeks as a logical paradox. The ancient representation of vagueness is the problem of the heap of sand. When you have a heap of sand, you have a relatively safe inference that if you take one grain from a heap, then you will still have a heap. Even in the strongest Stoic sense of logical consequence: the subsequent heap of sand is contained in the previous heap of sand. As the story goes, eventually taking grains of sand will show this if, then statement to be faulty because you will no longer have a heap of sand. Why does the "if, then" fail us here?

This question can be grappled with using different logics. Paraconsistent logic allows vagueness to occur without trivializing the entire logical system. Probability theory allows degrees of vagueness, and degrees of belief about vague situations. Constructive logic, from a practical view, has a more precise set of values than "true" and "false" (recognized to be vague terms), and from a theoretical view, begins with vagueness between "one" and "two", saying that these concepts need to be essentialized (the vagueness removed) before arithmetic can begin. (Brouwer 1981) All these logics are alive in research today. While logical pluralism doesn't solve the problem of vagueness, it is a direct response to vagueness. As the ancient logicians grappled with vagueness, so current logicians continue the struggle. (Beall & Restall 2006); (Weber 2010)

Using vagueness is an important skill that young people learn. (Rowland 2000) Rowland argues that vagueness has a positive effect when students learn to use it—to save face, to allow degrees of commitment in making mathematical conjectures, to say things (through the use of the vague and general word "it") without knowing the proper word (Channell 1994). Vague language in the classroom allows sensitivity to the vagueness of the content, in Rowland's case, of numbers.

It is the intent, through the use of physical stimuli, to show that vagueness is not an abstract problem, it is a physical 'embodied' problem; it is not removed from our common experience and understandings, vagueness is lived in constantly. The activity described below is a physical experiment that is designed to make students look at vagueness as a scientist might. How would students respond to a scientific 'experiment' activity that focuses on the physical manifestation of vagueness? Vagueness is usually recognized as a philosophical problem. The disciplines touched on in this multi-disciplinary study are physical science, math and philosophy.

Since it is already known that logical pluralism is possible because there are genuinely vague situations where more than one logic can give different and contradictory logical results, rather than focus on the logical side which is where much of the work continues, the conceptual work here will focus on exploring vagueness, a topic that is probably better left to poetry. After the conceptual exploration of vagueness, the web app purported to teach logical pluralism is presented, and another innovation meant as a way for young students to encounter vagueness is also presented.

Literature Review and Conceptual Work

2.1 What is vagueness

"It is a curious situation. There are legions of competing accounts of vagueness in the literature, and yet there appears to be no neutral description of what these theories are accounts of." (p4 Shapiro 2006) Ullmann (1972) argues that some writers, especially poets, consider vagueness an advantage to language, where logicians, mathematicians, and philosophers seem to think vagueness is a disadvantage. Ullmann points out that the term "vague" is vague, or ambiguous (p117-118) (although Russell (1923) gave one definition of vagueness as ambiguity: that there is more than one possible referent for a given word-use) Ullmann offers a disambiguation of the term vague, which includes the general.

On the other hand, Peirce is adamant that there be a clear distinction between general and vague. (reprinted in Peirce 1934). The indeterminacy of generality (general knowledge is a useful kind of knowledge) lies in variation within a class, while indeterminacy of vagueness lies at the boundaries of classes. (Rowland 2000, Kindle Locations 1697-1700) The distinction, it must be noticed, suffers from vagueness, because there are individuals that lie near the boundary of a class that may or may not also be one of the variations allowed by a generality. Not only is it easy to miss the difference between vagueness and generality, the difference may be vague.

Channell (1994) tries to describe the importance of vague use of subjects so connected:

> 2. Analysis of vague expressions shows that their meanings are themselves vague. By this I mean that it is not possible to turn them into something precise for the purpose of tidy analysis.

> 3. The results of elicitation tests indicated that the respondents all made similar judgements about vague expressions. Although they are vague, speakers share knowledge of how to understand them.

4. Vague expressions are not empty fillers, inserted by speakers to give processing time. They are deliberately chosen for their contribution to the communicative message.

5. Nor are vague expressions evidence of linguistic inadequacy on the part of the speaker or writer. They are part of the linguistic repertoire of the competent language user...

6. Vague language is not bad or wrong, but nor is it inherently good. Its use needs to be considered with reference to contexts and situations.."p196-197 "12. Vague language is a broad and fruitful area of language study, with considerable potential for further work." (Channell 1994, p198)

Channell and Rowland argue that vagueness has pragmatic usefulness: "For language to be fully useful, therefore, in the sense of being able to describe all of human beings' experience, it must incorporate built-in flexibility. This flexibility resides, in part, in its capacity for vagueness." (p201 Channell 1994) Dr. Channell outlines various views of where vagueness comes from, from the difference between the "same idea" in different minds (Fodor 1977 in Channell 1994), to language (Peirce 1902 in Channell 1994), to physical reality (Russell 1923). Vagueness is found discussed in logic (Lakoff 1972 in Channell 1994) where it is argued (along with Russell) that "true" and "false" are vague, and so classical logic could be modified to create other logics, such as probability theory. There are many other alternatives for logic; all stem from the troubling properties of vagueness.

"[i]t is perfectly obvious, since colours form a continuum, that there are shades of colour concerning which we shall be in doubt whether to call them red or not, not because we are ignorant of the meaning of the word "red," but because it is a word the extent of whose application is essentially doubtful." (1923 Russell).

The word "red" is vague in this respect because there are borderline cases where it is not clear whether or not we should call the case "red". Russell says "essentially doubtful" because this uncertainty is essential, in the sense of being a part of the nature of "red". One deception here is in asserting that the "continuum" is perfectly precise, that underneath vague words is a perfectly precise reality that can be expressed numerically. This renders vagueness a kind of error; without a perfectly known continuum underneath our words, vagueness is not error but has a reality of its own. Does the continuum suffer from vagueness? My purpose here is explore different definitions of vagueness and review distinctions between similar concepts such as underspecificity and generality.

Keefe (2000, p 10) writes that 'X is an integer greater than thirty' is not vague because it has sharp boundaries. However there are a number of integers it could be, so we call it "underspecific". There seems to be a relationship between underspecificity and generality. The statement "an integer greater than 30" is general in the same way that it is underspecific. As far as underspecificity, first of all, we rely heavily on the definition of an integer. If we were talking about real numbers, this example would suffer from vagueness, even though real numbers are more precise at pinpointing a real position than integers. For example, suppose I meant by writing:
3.1415...
That I am talking about a number between 3.14159999999... and 3.14150000000....

Is 3.1415... vague? At least, a number between 3.141599999... and 3.141500000 is both general and vague. It is general because there are many numbers that could be chosen from this range. It is vague because if the number chosen is near enough to one of the borders (3.15159999... or 3.14150000...) we are not sure if the number is properly inside the range, or outside the borders.

Peirce claimed that another way to describe generality is where the Law of Excluded Middle ("A or ~A is always true") does not hold. This makes sense because normally, the LEM decides which of "A or ~A" is true (even if we don't know which is decided, it asserts that "out there" it is decided.) When the LEM does not apply "A or ~A" is left undecided, which allows for a generalization on "A or ~A", you can choose which. However the claim that something can be essentially uncertain, is directly against the LEM.

The description 'a number between 3.14159999999... and 3.14150000000....' is vague because I cannot assume that I can write "9"s or "0"s forever, and if I left the job of writing this to my children and grandchildren, there is no telling when one of them would rebel against the task. The question of whether or not the "..." settles anything about what a real number actually is, is purely a rhetorical question. There is no mathematical basis for either claim. Here is a better parallel from Wittgenstein:

"Suppose we divide to thirty places, and someone says we needn't divide but only copy after the first six places. You could say, "How on earth can a logical proof be shortened? Either you have to divide or you needn't divide. If we just copy out the figures, then we do not divide in the old way any more."—If we say the proof that the first thirty places are so-and-so is given by dividing, then isn't it queer that this can be shortened? Either this is the proof—but then it must be given: how can we leave out a part of the proof and still get the proof? Did we at first do something superfluous? If its a logical proof, then that alone should justify the conclusion. To say something else can justify it seems to make logic rather arbitrary. Surely you can see we needn't go on"—all I know is that you won't go on. If you leave off dividing and do something else instead, what is it that you have shown? Now Watson said we believe that copying this will do. Will do for what? What trick is it supposed to do?" (Wittgenstein 1976, p125 my emphasis)

Assuming the continuum were perfectly known and not vague, how would we refer one of its numbers? The word "one" is still vague (or in Keefe's case "30") in the same sense that "a heap" is vague, or "red" is vague, taking away grains (or 0.000... 0100000... away from 1) and we don't know when we will not have a heap (one) anymore. Now at least practically this is true, if you have one apple and you take away this tiny speck of the apple, it is still one apple, but why should the abstracted number "one" be different from our experience? And when it is abstracted, how can we make the claim that the number is "real"?

The distinction between underspecificity and vagueness, when it applies to real things with more troubling boundaries than integers, is only possible if we imagine a limitless amount of knowledge about the continuum, that it is comprised of perfectly precise and known positions that can fall underneath any vague term, as Russell invites us to imagine by saying the colors fall on a "continuum" and comparing that term for color to the term "red". Russell's definition of vagueness: "Per contra, a representation is vague when the relation of the representing system to the represented system is not one-one, but one-many"

Under this definition "3.1415..." is not vague, because it is claimed by the completeness axiom that the least upper bound of this sequence is least, and therefore unique (and a number). This is the same as assuming the continuum is perfectly known, at least known well enough to assert an ordering principle to "real" space. Russell uses this definition to claim that all language is vague, and if the continuum is "known" in the sense of the axiom of completeness, then of course any word (such as apple) is not only vague but indefinitely so (keep removing tiny specks of apple). Imagining a mysterious field of perfect precision actually creates vagueness from a practical view of language-use.

"But wherever degree or any other possibility of continuous variation subsists, absolute precision is impossible. Much else must be vague, because no man's interpretation of words is based on exactly the same experience as any other man's. Even in our most intellectual conceptions, the more we strive to be precise, the more unattainable precision seems. It should never be forgotten that our own thinking is carried on as a dialogue, and though mostly to a lesser degree, is subject to almost every imperfection of language." (Peirce 1960, p506, my emphasis)

He is saying that things like the continuum, "one" (and 30) are vague, his concept of the continuum, "our most intellectual conception" is not at all one of limitless knowledge. The theory of real numbers needs to be reformulated. Rather, the basic fabric of things is not an imagined field of perfect precision, but a dialogue, whether it be internal or external.

"he[Kempe] means to exclude distinction by means of relations. All this is utterly paradoxical to the logician, who will say that two vertices of a square are distinguished from each other in not being opposite the same vertex, and in various other ways. But the difficulty disappears as soon as he recognizes that Kempe's units are not supposed to be real objects, but are only vague ideas, to which nobody ever supposed the principle of contradiction to apply." (Peirce 1960, p505)

Peirce defines vagueness as the situation where the principle of contradiction doesn't apply. Aristotle's version of the principle of contradiction is that "A is B" and "A is not B" are mutually exclusive. Peirce's definition makes sense because, in borderline cases where A is between "B" and "~B" whether or not "A is B" or "A is not B" is not clear.

Analytically, the continuum fails to dispel vagueness, what about empirical investigation? Russell defines vagueness as a particular case of the general law of physics that as things get more distant (or smaller), they become indistinct. So we may refer to "Saturn's rings" and wonder if they are real, since one "ring" actually refers to many drifting rocks and only appears in the shape of a ring. Still, the rocks are made of particles, and only appear as rocks, etc. What we are left with is an impasse between appearances and an ever-elusive smallest particle. Vagueness sits at the edge of our knowledge, just beyond the smallest particle we can be aware of. Which is considered knowledge, or where do we rest after investigation—on the knowledge of smallest particles or on the vagueness that allows these particles to appear?

2.2 Addressing theories that try to solve vagueness Shapiro chooses a pragmatic definition of vagueness, where people, "competent speakers" of the language, come to a consensus on what a vague word means, or how it is applied to an "open" case, that is, a case that competent speakers can differ in opinion (before reaching consensus) without calling their competence into question. These competent speakers are the "masters" of the meaning of a word, and he recognizes that choosing a competent speaker may be a vague problem itself. Waisman believed that a vague concept must have unlegislated cases where "established meanings and non-linguistic facts allow" one to go either way on the matter. (Shapiro 2006, Loc 3729-3733)

Shapiro uses an example called the "forced march" to display the power of his theory to handle vagueness with "competent speakers." The forced march is done by a group of such speakers who examine the hair on the heads of 2000 men arrayed from entirely bald and progressing gradually to Jerry Garcia. They must reach a consensus each time, and Shapiro is concerned with the eventuality that, starting with Jerry Garcia, and inferring that a a small tuft of hair less on the next man preserves hairiness, the inference will break down and the competent speakers, one by one, will be filled with conflict until they decide that one of the men is bald (well before they get to the entirely bald man at the other end of this continuation). Shapiro argues that on breaking the inference with a particular man (lets call this man B(a)), classical logic requires that this break spreads to the men near B(a), so they are now also "bald" even though some of them were only a moment before considered "not bald." Interestingly where exactly this spread of baldness around B(a) ends, and end it must before Jerry Garcia, is unknown, or deferred to further investigation. Needless to say, the deliberation of competent speakers on which men are bald and which men are not is never-ending. Instead of admitting that logic is wrong, we are directed to work and deliberate on the problem forever, and if we ever throw up our hands and stop working, the consistency of classical logic would be questionable.

However, despite this shortcoming in Shapiro's theory, he is sensitive to how difficult vagueness is to solve. He notices that the progression from one man to the other may be imperceptible in how much hair they have. Going from one man to the next, the decision of bald or not is not done by comparison to the previous man—in truly tough vague situations there is no perceivable difference between the two. So the comparison has to happen between someone further up the march.

It seems that the experience of motion or time is sensed with memory, because given sufficiently small enough time intervals, any motion through time is imperceptibly different, effectively the same. All motion is vague in this sense, and it may be that the problem of vagueness is just the "hard" problem of motion. When we move from short to tall or from child to adult, we must traverse a vague borderline. As such, Zeno's paradoxes of motion, which can be taken as the contradictions one encounters when trying to describe motion with points, are quite relevant to the vagueness. That our words are vague simply means that they are in motion.

Motion is found to trouble another theory: supervaluationism, which is one powerful solution to vagueness that preserves classical logic. Its slogan is "truth is super-truth." Super-truth is an analysis of a situation where all precisifications of the situation are clear cases. When there is no vagueness, then we know what is true. In a vague situation where some precisifications yield one result and other precifications yield other results, a relevant proposition is not super-true, so it is not true. One problem with such an account is the idea that precisifications of a vague situation shift and are not absolute.

> "The supposedly precise extensions of the predicates can change in the very act of our considering them as we go through an argument, trying to reason in an ordinary situation. We might call this a Heraclitus problem. Just as the river changes every time we step into it, the extensions of vague predicates change momentarily, literally right before our eyes. An argument may be valid, and its premises might be true at a given moment, but by the time a human reasoner has concluded something on the basis of them, the extension of the terms may have changed, and along with that, some of the sentences may no longer be true. It is small comfort to learn that the conclusion was true." (Shapiro 2006, Loc 656-661)

This is in support of vagueness as just a manifestation of the "hard" problem of motion: motion of language. To hold that language, including logical language, moves is to trouble Aristotle's fundamental doctrine that form determines validity. If logical language moves, its form wont stay still and the forms that determine validity (forms of language), become moving targets. One true logic cannot deal with such a difficult problem because the logical language will eventually shift away from what is actually valid. Vagueness is a deep and persistent problem for mathematicians that generate very long formal proofs.

In this sense, vagueness is in a near-opposite relationship with form, or it is the result of the opposing relationship between form and substance. The claim that logic can "solve" vagueness is the claim that ultimately substance doesn't exist.
Frege (1879) shed light on how technical language is opposed to vagueness.

> "I can best make the relation of my ideography to ordinary language dear if I compare it to that which the microscope has to the ordinary eye ... Considered as an optical instrument, [the eye] exhibits many imperfections, which ordinarily remain unnoticed ... [A]s soon as scientific goals demand great sharpness of resolution, the eye proves to be insufficient. (Frege 1879: Preface)" (as quoted in Shapiro 2006, Loc 850-855)

This quote by Frege is very important and shows the tension between vagueness and logic. Vagueness is a result of a lack of magnification, "sharpness of resolution" required for scientific investigation is an abundance of magnification. Shapiro thinks that Frege is a realist in saying this, but why is demanding ever-more sharp resolutions realistic? It seems that Frege is insisting that whatever we find in our investigations is not enough, that any reality sensed, either with the eye or instruments, is not actually real, but we must refine our instruments to look ever-deeper. The end of such a story is not an affirmation of reality, but a fixed dissatisfaction with any vague substantive being that shifts into view under the microscope.

Modern mathematical logic does not address vagueness in any explicit way. Shapiro believes that "there is no vagueness in mathematics (or so it seems)" (Shapiro 2006 loc 863-865) Vagueness is still in the languages of mathematics: as in Shapiro's "forced march" or the march of the decimal digits of pi, vagueness is deferred to more investigation in the future.

> Like it or not, vagueness is here to stay. It is part of the way we deal with the world via language. Given the sorts of beings we are, we have to deal with the world this way (see e.g. Wright 1976, and Ch. 7). Thus, there is not much point in trying to use a precise language instead of English, or to pretend that one is not using a vague language, or to look forward to the day when we no longer use such a language. I thus reject the normative orientation, at least concerning vagueness." (Shapiro 2006, Loc 875-878)

Shapiro argues that vagueness should be modeled with a precise mathematical language. He says that such a language-model is descriptive, not normative. However, he insists on a precise mathematical language, not English, even though the above quote seems to suggest otherwise. He wants to model vagueness with tools that, merely by being used, abstract vagueness, the thing to be studied, out before it can be studied. Shapiro is aware of this difficulty. He defines representors of a model as parts of the model that are close to reality (in this case, natural vague languages like English). Artifacts are parts of a model that are not close to reality.

> "Rosanna Keefe [2000: Ch. 2] points out that ...When it comes to vague languages, the advocate of a given model must show just which features of the model are artifacts and which are representors, and show how the sorites paradox is resolved in terms of the representors. It is not fair to present a model that supposedly resolves the sorites paradox, but then not accept the very features of the model that resolve the paradox." (Shapiro 2006, Loc 950-953)

Classical logic uses the Law of Excluded Middle: that there is no vagueness between a "p" and a "not-p." When it comes to modeling vagueness, this is definitely an artifact.

> "We have no initial reason to think that excluded middle holds. Perhaps it is the direct opposite. Borderline cases at least seem to be failures of bivalence, which underlies classical semantics. Moreover, bivalence is connected with excluded middle via the truth schemes..." (Shapiro 2006, Loc 988-995)

The idea that a logic of vagueness is a meta -language, meant to model a natural language such as English has many problems. One is the logic of vagueness (likely) contains vagueness. It would not do to claim to describe vagueness precisely, if the model just uses vague indeterminacies for the job. If any vagueness is found in the meta-language (once it is developed), it should be described, but this would require a meta-meta language to describe it. Wittgenstein took the pragmatic route and set this problem aside, saying that climbing from meta to meta-meta, etc. languages is not practical, eventually we just have to act using the languages we have created the best way we can.

> "We do not know, for example, whether every instance of P or not P is counted true in our language and thought, and one pertinent reason for this doubt stems from vagueness." (Sainsbury 1990, §7)

The law of excluded middle is a very strong assumption that seems to do away with any vagueness, for, as in any sorites situation, the question is between "p or not-p" e.g. "bald or not-bald." Asserting that it must be the case one way or the other is to insist that vagueness is not a real problem, it is to ignore it, not describe it. However Shapiro assumes:

...without argument, that the logic for this theory is classical, with apologies to my intuitionistic friends and opponents. As Kamp put it, "such is the classical theory of sets". This precise, classical framework is employed to model the semantics and logic of a vague object language. I realize that by doing it this way, I cannot get things exactly right. " (Shapiro 2006 loc 1007-1026)

Words are alive in the sense that the living live (not use) in them, and repurpose them, ultimately for the happiness of the living. All Shapiro can offer to console humanity engaged in his "forced march" is "thats life." (Shapiro 2006 Kindle Locations 468-472) Life is supposed to be hard. Happiness is only attained through hard work, under the prescriptions of Aristotle's logic (and other great minds). And where is Shapiro in this scheme of hard work? He is one of the "masters." Evoking Humpty Dumpty talking to Alice, Shapiro claims that the meaning of words, at least in vague situations, is decided by the "masters."

He goes further in his last chapter where he blusters and complains about the problem of whether vagueness is real or illusory. He says that calling vagueness real is "metaphysical vagueness." If vagueness were real, then of course it wouldn't matter what competent speakers decide on the matter, the matter would remain vague in actuality. "Is it possible for the extension of a mind-independent PROPERTY to be dependent on the judgments of competent speakers of a natural language, even in part? Are human judgments that much in tune with the ultimate constituents of REALITY? This query is, of course, in line with the impatience with metaphysical vagueness that I expressed in the previous section." (Shapiro 2006, Loc 3465-3467) Bluster aside, the second question is actually astute, and here it is accepted that we see vague things and speak vague words because vagueness is real.

It does not take so much attunement to recognize that vagueness is apparent everywhere. It may be hard for some to snap out of their years of mathematical education on precise things and look at the world, and give themselves the tiny bit of authority that is required to let them believe what they sense. Shapiro is trying to get our minds into his particular yoga pose that makes out vagueness as not a real phenomenon, something to be worked against (forever). And if we don't read his book and display our yoga prowess, then we shouldn't be allowed to talk about or accept what is readily available to our senses, instead we should submit to the rule of the "masters".

To get an idea about this yoga pose, contrast Shapiro's first question (above) with this statement at the beginning of his book. "The present view is that vagueness turns on judgment-dependence. If there is no judgment-dependence, then there is no vagueness." (Shapiro 2006, Loc 754) So which is it? Are vague things judgement dependent, in which case whether something is or isn't "red" is to be decided by the "masters," or is it impossible for "a mind-independent PROPERTY to be dependent on the judgments of competent speakers" Shapiro says that his book only deals with vagueness that is judgement-dependent. He admits there may be vagueness that is not judgement-dependent, and his book does not deal with this kind of vagueness. (ibid 804-807). Ultimately Shapiro sides with pragmatics on the issue, that is, he puts the question aside and focuses on deciding vague contexts when it is useful to do so. Competent speakers make a decision, but that doesn't change the actual physical situation, the decision changes the social situation (such as the consensus - seeking forced march). Obviously getting it right is usually more useful than not, but ascribing the correct property is not the issue, doing your job as it is prescribed is the issue. However there is serious tension between what is social and what is physical; a tension that is a fundamental aspect of social constructivism. This tension between whether or not vagueness is (actually) judgement-dependent runs through the whole book.

Shapiro also notices that his "forced march" is (at least to him) an ideal situation for vagueness. Most vagueness goes unrelegated by a group of competent speakers. We are lucky if a vague situation has one competent speaker, and even luckier if we happen to know for sure that the speaker is competent or not.

With that, I leave Shapiro. He assumes the logic for this theory is classical, and chooses to ignore how vagueness is in direct tension with this decision. He at least knows what he is doing, but to insist on a model for vagueness, using a "sharp" tool that assumes phenomena (or predicates) to be the opposite of what you are trying to model with those tools, is not a very appealing approach. Vagueness naturally avoids such an attempt and avoids it completely. In the end, another logic can crop up that will be better. I do agree that context is important, or a situation, to the problem of which logic to use. But the spirit of this agreement points directly away from having just one logic or model to use or to understand with.

2.3 Higher-order vagueness

"sorites[vagueness] ... is solved independently of any particular meaning analysis of the predicate ... On the contrary, all that is required to solve the puzzle is a claim about the correct application or extension ... of the predicate at issue." ... 'I do not claim that the meaning analysis or intension of a vague predicate includes a judgmental element. For instance, I do not claim that in calling an object red one means or is saying, in either the "speaker" or "semantic" sense, that the object is merely red-relative- to-me-now or red-relative-to-such- and-such-a-context ... Rather, I claim that the extension of "red"-the class of objects that satisfy the predicate-is always r e l a t i v i z e d t o c e r t a i n p s y c h o l o g i c a l (a n d nonpsychological) contexts. The sorites is a puzzle about the correct application of vague predicates, and that is all my story addresses. (Raffman 1994, p 66)"

Sometimes, "what is red" requires a judgement call, that is, the extension of red, or how "red" is to be applied, requires a judgement call. Raffman is saying this requirement does not mean "what red is" requires a judgement call. However, this ignores the problem of higher-order vagueness. The judgement calls on "what is red" effects the ultimate understanding of "what red is." That means that what red is and what is red are interdependent. Whether our "masters" confirm their competence in a non-vague situation, or exercise their competence as the master of meaning in a vague situation, is vague, because the difference between a vague and non-vague situation is vague.

> "For one thing, to speak of the ordinary use of language is ... questionable, implying as it does, that there is such a thing, and a unique one, and that one can find out what it is. But how ought one to determine what this ordinary use is, e.g., in a case of doubt? What ought one to do-to ask people? Any people? Or only the competent ones? And who is to decide who is "competent"-the leading circles of society, the experts of language, the writers just in vogue? And supposing there are people generally considered competent-what what if they disagree?' (Waismann 1951b, p 122)

After some levels of higher order vagueness (beyond the third level), it is deemed not pragmatic to consider yet higher orders of vagueness. If there is no pragmatic existence of higher order vagueness because language-users don't make sense of the third level or beyond, that turns on whether there actually is vagueness, and hence higher order vagueness. If there is, then it is the job of language-users to overcome their limitations in order to shed light on it. The pragmatic account of higher-order vagueness depends on the metaphysical status of vagueness: whether it is real or not.

The super-valuationist also has trouble with higher-order vagueness. Keefe's (2000) solution: to use a vague meta-language, which is basically to accept higher-order vagueness (maybe to shed light on it) without solving it.

"when we make enough concessive assumptions to have an intelligible thesis of [metaphysical] vagueness, we have a thesis which can be shown to be false by a few short lines of proof", namely the short argument in Evans [1978]." The thesis of metaphysical vagueness is that vagueness is real, supported here. The idea that such a thesis can be logically disproven puts logic before vagueness. However it should be put the other way around. Vagueness is prior to logic—this is exactly Beall's claim that logical consequence is vague, and therefore gives rise to logical pluralism. Which logic disproves vagueness? Just the logic that, before it begins, assumes away the existence of vagueness, and with it the world. Evans argument assumes that there cannot be an "A" that is both indeterminate and not indeterminate, which is just evoking the law of excluded middle, exactly the assumption that assumes away vagueness. Making our thoughts agree with the vague experience of the senses is imperative for understanding, it cannot be ignored simply because vague sense data is "unintelligible". Vagueness is not a logical doctrine, it does not need to be proven. It is an empirical fact. The fact that every human observation is vague carries its own strength. Only a great deal of sitting in a schoolroom can get people to not notice it in favor of logic.

Authors are apt to assume metaphysical doctrines that seem to "clean up" vagueness, but not to endorse vagueness: Williamson (1994), an epistemist, argues that in borderline cases there are actual break points between "bald" and "not-bald," its just that we can't know where that borderline is. Delia Graff (2001) argues that vague situations have sharp borders, but they merely shift out of sight when we look for them. The investigation itself changes the context for subsequent investigation. We never see the sharp borderline, yet it is there, and if we look for it, it shifts out of our sight. Such a metaphysical assumption is akin to believing that knowledge is knowable because transcendental forces conspire for us to know. This is much harder to swallow than the thesis that what we sense is vague because vagueness is (metaphysically?) real.

2.4 What Vagueness is not

Even though vagueness and nonvagueness contaminate each other, there are some things that vagueness is not and nonvagueness is. Vagueness is not substance, when a heap of sand is clearly a heap, it still has substance, but it is not vague. Likewise when enough grains have been removed that we are sure it is not a heap anymore, what remains has substance, but is not vague. Vagueness is still potentially everywhere, since there can always be some question whether we have used the right word/formula to describe substance. Vagueness is what thwarts an attempt to formulate substance (the continuum is such an attempt).

It amounts to saying that substance can't be formulated. The ignorance of what substance is, since it can't be formulated, is what makes substance a pure potential. When we try to know substance by formula or theory, vagueness ensures that our formula is not complete, even in non-vague situations, there is still vague phenomena on the blurry edges of our theory. Take the heap of sand, in a situation where it is non-vague, where we clearly still have a heap, there are grains that are so small in our heap as to be barely detectable, and may or may not qualify to be called a grain to be removed. In any scientific theory, no matter how clear, vagueness is there; as the grain of sand is like any word, it has borderlines for how the word should be used (language), or what is a grain (reality).

But vagueness is not everything, the way substance is. And I have claimed that questions are the linguistic expression of vagueness, but really questions are the linguistic expression of substance, and vagueness is tightly linked to substance when scientific investigation is underway, that is, converting substance into formulae (incompletely). What is the relationship between substance and vagueness during scientific investigation? Vagueness is a kind of substance, that is, a kind of substance that no longer "stands underneath". It is instead at the edges of word and matter, bordering on being outside a form. Vagueness is when substance is released from word and matter, becoming a pure potential that is (almost) outside the game of formulation, outside the scientific excavation of substance

Vagueness is when raw experience spills over the word-containers we use to capture/describe said experience. In that sense it is substance, but only in that particular situation of the chase and capture of raw experience with words. Vagueness requires inquiry to arise, but it is constituted by the real world, it is not constituted by words. This can be seen when we arrive at the vague situation of our "heap" of sand. Heap doesn't describe it anymore (or does it?) but for sure there is still an experience. This experience fails to fall into a category, it can only be experienced, not recognized. Vagueness is not the embodiment of ignorance or uncertainty, because vagueness depends on inquiry to exist. As will be explored in the conclusion, vagueness is the body of inquiry. Vagueness requires earnest searching with the senses (including the mind), and grasping with words, to inquire.

2.5 Meaning, Vagueness, Truth

I have used vagueness in a lot of ways. This is the definition of vagueness I want to use for the purposes of pointing to logical pluralism.
The vague might be defined as that to which the principle of contradiction does not apply." (Peirce 1960, 505)

Wandering among different definitions (vague comes from the Latin vagus which means to wander), the roads seemed to converge to Russell's definition of vagueness, when a word leads its user towards more than one applicable meaning, . Russell (And I) used this definition to argue that all language is vague, language is a "garden of forking paths" to quote Borge's story about a book that actually succeeds in chronicling the passage of time, forking as all possible choices are made. Russell noticed that these paths can be seen in experience—as things come closer, a multitude of details become available, all calling us to follow them. Sometimes I refer to this "general law of physics" (Russell 1923) as vagueness, even though Russell did not intend for that.

However I will attempt to show that Peirce's definition is equivalent to these other definitions and generalizations. The principle of contradiction fails when you can't tell if "A is B" or "A is not B". So in the case when you are looking at a star in the sky through a telescope, and you can almost make out that it looks like two stars close together, we can say that "that light is one star" or "that light is two stars". Holding both these statements is classically illogical by noncontradiction, and both can be held because the situation is vague—both in Peirce's sense and Russell's physical law. So Peirce's definition can be applied to Russell's general law over vagueness, and this can be applied to the particular law Russell gives for vagueness as well, because when a word has two or more applicable meanings, for example "The gray sky…" and the readers are unsure if I mean the color or a dismal feeling. In this case "gray is the color" and "gray is the dismal feeling" fit into Peirce's definition of "A is B" or "A is not B" failing.

What about the borderline case? Some writers (Keefe 2007) assert that vagueness is exclusively found when we run into fuzzy borders. However, as in Keefe, these fuzzy borders are held to be neither true nor false (close to a failure of noncontradiction) because on closer inspection, or by making the word more precise, some precifications favor one side of the border while others precifications favor the other. This is exactly Russell's "ambiguous" definition of vagueness—a situation where a word could have more than one meaning. When we "look" more closely, or inquire with greater sensitivity, precifications come into "focus." Keefe distinguishes ambiguous from vague, while other authors try to join them.

The wandering cannot take place without inquiry, the looking at phenomena and noticing details. Then physically following/recognizing some details over others. Its not that wandering is merely a possibility that troubles what we know. We actually wander when we inquire, and if there is no wandering— if, say, we are following a mathematical calculation with set rules and a right answer, this is not inquiry.

2.5.1 What is meaning?

There are some famous quips about the slipperiness of the term meaning. Quine said:

> Pending a satisfactory explanation of the notion of meaning, linguists in semantic fields are in the situation of not knowing what they are talking about." (Quine 1961 p 47)

What could meaning mean? How do we mean the meaning of meaning? I have seen the term used ambiguously as in

> "A good theory is very mean with what it supposes there to be." (Gregory 2017, p 19)

One of the problems is that meaning has opposite meanings which are often confused. Sometimes when people ask for meaning, they are asking for Lipman's idea that meaning is a whole-part relationship.

"For example, suppose you had planned to go to a movie with some friends, but you got there late—just in time for the last scene, by which you were completely bewildered. So you turn to your friends, as the lights come up, and you say, "What did it mean? What did it mean?" They tell you all that had happened before your arrival—and suddenly the last scene snaps into place. Its meaning becomes clear to you as you see it as a part of a larger whole." (Lipman & Sharp 1980, loc 576)

The utterance or stimulus at hand is the part, and how it relates to so many other things, to the rest of the world, even, is its meaning. That's one meaning of meaning.

Another totally opposite meaning of meaning is Russell's use of the word, where you are looking for a particular (and single) referent to apply the word.

the would-be one-one relation between the representing system and the represented system will be meaning. In an accurate language, meaning would be a one-one relation; no word would have two meanings, and no two words would have the same meaning. In actual languages, as we have seen, meaning is one-many. … That is to say, there is not only one object that a word means, and not only one possible fact that will verify a proposition. The fact that meaning is a one-many relation is the precise statement of the fact that all language is more or less vague." (Russell 1923)

In this case instead of lateral relationships, you are focusing the word towards an external referent. One meaning of meaning explodes the word to its relationships towards a larger whole, the other focuses the meaning of meaning to an even smaller (and external) part of what is said. Of course, looking more closely at such a focus will reveal that there is always vagueness (or ambiguity) no matter how well we focus. But such a focus can be pragmatically settled, ultimately a marriage of the two meanings of meanings is necessary for pragmatic "use". So when someone asks you "what do you mean?" even though it is a very pointed(or explosive?) question, one you should obviously be able to answer, the question is at odds with itself.

2.5.2 What is Truth?

These two meanings of meaning have a parallel in the two dominant logical theories of truth. The coherence theory of truth does not suppose an external reality (nor does it exclude the possibility of realism). A proposition gets its truth from the other propositions of the logic. If the other true propositions of a set are consistent with a new proposition, and usually some other conditions such as, for example, some kind of entailment of the new proposition, then the new proposition is true. That is the coherence theory(s) of truth. Note the similarity to the idea of meaning being its relationship to a larger whole.

The correspondence theory of truth, on the other hand, asserts that there is a real, unthinking and unthought of world that "satisfies" a proposition about this real world. Then the proposition is true. So when you say a word you mean a specific thing, not its relationship to the rest of the world/conversation/etc. Of course this is parallel to the meaning of meaning that focuses towards an external referent.

2.5.3 Truth, Meaning, Vagueness

Now, what do I mean by meaning? I think vagueness is a concept that can heal the divide between the two meanings of meaning and the two theories of truth. For one thing, we can be talking about something small, such as quantum-level probabilities, even then there isn't just one thing or particle we are talking about. In the case of "The gray sky" vagueness is an advantage to the poet who wishes to blur, as a painter blurs a reflection on the water. What does he mean by "The gray sky"? If you are searching for a decision on whether it be color or a dismal feeling, you'll search in vain. Here the poet doesn't totally reject the correspondence theory of truth though. Couldn't he mean both and still be pointing to "one thing"? And how does this sit with the coherence theory, if the poet moved our reader from searching for a decision on whether he means the color or the feeling to accepting both, he has won a small victory in favor of meaning being a part-whole relationship, he has also put an end to the assertion that all language is vague.

The failure of the scientist is the success of the poet. A larger whole "both feeling and color" has been discovered or created. The key question is, given that the continuum is pending reformulation, could this larger whole be "really" only one thing, and therefore not vague? (Assuming the current continuum creates vagueness for all our "normal" words.) Maybe there is a certain force to the idea that a gray sky (color) is fused with a dismal feeling, a consistency. And this force, consistency, while far from logical entailment, lends its strength to a coherence theory of truth and the correspondence theory. We started with the vagueness of the term "gray sky," and by fusing the meanings, made the term refer to only one thing, so that our meaning corresponds to one object.

> "'It is also necessary that you should not always choose the right word: there is nothing more precious than the grey song where Vagueness and Precision meet.'" (Verlaine "Art poetique" as quoted and translated by Ullmann 1972, p117)

Vagueness in the classroom looks like this:

> the Lipmanian discussion plan tends to approach concept-work through analogical reasoning and categorical play. It seeks to render the concept 'fuzzy'— to push it beyond the boundaries of its conventional use through a sort of poetics of instantiation: the concept is applied beyond its familiar denotation through playing with its extensional possibilities, which sets up a dialectical relation between the 'literal' and the metaphorical." (Kennedy & Kennedy 2011, loc 3303-3320 (my emphasis))

Two concepts that can be "pushed beyond their boundaries" is "truth" and "meaning", since they are vague (they could mean the coherence or the correspondence theory). Rendering a concept fuzzy is done by looking at it closely to see how it could be applied in a "one-to-many" way, and then wondering, not just "which of these "many" is meant?", also "do we mean a fusion of some of these meanings?". When trying to determine if a proposition is true, we need not look at all possible precifications as in the super-valuation theory of vagueness. Instead we can fuse those precifications that we think are meant by the proposition. This at first glance appears as not a universal approach to truth and meaning. It puts a universal power in the hands of the communicators, rather than asserting a universal that communicators have no say in.

A concept can also be rendered fuzzy by looking at its borderlines with other concepts, its relationships to the rest of language. Most importantly, looking closely within a concept for its meaning, and looking around a concept, at its boundaries, are rendered the same activity: looking for vagueness. The two senses of meaning, though opposite, can be rendered vague. As in the example of "gray sky." Looking to the boundary between the word and an external referent, when we see that there could be more than one referent, and these different referents are effectively "fused" or "confused" in vagueness. Likewise, when the boundaries of "gray sky" are rendered vague, such as with a fogged-over horizon and a reflecting ocean, the ocean and the gray sky are partly "fused" or "confused". This is the same activity for both meanings of meaning.

logical propositions also, so far as we can know them, become vague through the vagueness of "truth" and "falsehood"...Hence we are able to imagine a precise meaning for such words as "or" and "not". We can, in fact, see precisely what they would mean if our symbolism were precise. All traditional logic habitually assumes that precise symbols are being employed. It is therefore not applicable to this terrestrial life, but only to an imagined celestial existence...We are able to conceive precision; indeed, if we could not do so, we could not conceive vagueness, which is merely the contrary of precision." (Russell 1923)

Here we are back to the beginning wondering what vagueness is. Is the contrary to precision really the same as Peirce's definition that the law of non-contradiction fails? And if so, doesn't that mean that the law of non-contradiction is essentially the principle that precision is a fundamental ideal in logic? This would mean that one foundational enterprise of logic is to make things precise. (This will be explored more with Peirce's logic graphs) It is not that, as Aristotle would have it, each situation calls for the appropriate amount of precision, rather, unless we want to be accused of being illogical and therefore beneath reproach, logic is the enterprise of stamping out all vagueness, all metaphor, and entering Russell's "celestial existence" of precision. Such a belief clearly favors the focusing theories of truth and meaning. However, the strength of the coherence theories loom large—how can we know what things mean without knowing how it relates to the larger whole of our everyday lives? And how our lives are a part of something larger? A further consequence of recognizing vagueness as the contrary to precision is that vagueness is just another word for Foucault's "similitude"

"Only prudence on the part of the mind can dissipate them [similitudes], if it abjures its natural haste and levity in order to become 'penetrating' and ultimately perceive the differences inherent in nature." (F. Bacon Novum Organum book 1xlv and lix, as quoted in Foucault 1973, p52)

> "Bacon does not dissipate similitudes by means of evidence and its attendant rules. He shows them, shimmering before our eyes, vanishing as one draws near, then re-forming again a moment later, a little further off. They are idols." (Foucault 1973, p51)

> "Similitude is no longer the form of knowledge but rather the occasion of error." (Foucault 1973, p51)

Vagueness, with its unfortunate modern negative connotation, was similitude, what "vanishes as one draws near." Similitude was not an error, not darkness or the result of laziness, it was the very source of knowledge. Bacon set forth the project of Enlightenment which many are still driving towards. And vagueness does have this property of disappearing when you look more closely, at least until it is no longer possible or interesting to continue looking more closely, there vagueness remains undispelled. At this "limit of our knowledge" as we must refer to it under the current regime of thinking that precision is knowledge, we find, not individuals that are made by a poetic fusion, calling an end to our work, but a confusion of (meaningless?) information. It need not be so.

2.6 Entwining logical pluralism and vagueness in inquiry

Logical pluralism arises when a distinction (the fundamental logical activity is to make things precise by making distinctions) suffers from vagueness. The most basic situation is when it is unclear whether we have "A" or "~A". Since it is not "A or ~A", that is, since it is not true that it must be either A or ~A, because we may be in a vague situation, we have "A and ~A" by classical Demorgan's Law. It seems that an insensitive treatment of vagueness allows "A and ~A" to be true, and a more sensitive treatment of vagueness allows "A or ~A" to be false.

In logical theory, the rigidity and hence apparent finality of contrary propositions is often enforced by use of symbols that have no meaning or content of their own. A and Not-A are, for example, such symbols. These purely formalistic contraries cannot possibly have directive force. For if, say, "virtue" be assigned to A as its meaning, then Not- A includes not only vice but triangles, horse races, symphonies and the precession of the equinoxes. Since the time of Aristotle, the nugatory nature of "infinitation of the negative" has been generally recognized. What has not been so generally recognized is (1) that failure to recognize the intermediary function of contrary proposition tends in the direction of infinitation, and (2) that any purely formalistic either-or formulation of contraries (such as A and Not-A) eliminates reference to any universe of discourse and, hence, when any value is assigned to the positive expression, renders the negative wholly indeterminate. Nevertheless, the institution of opposites in hypothetical form, when interpreted as a means of fixing the limits within which determinate disjunctive alternatives fall, is a necessary preparatory logical procedure. (Dewey 1938, Loc 3292-3300)

"A or ~A" is just the beginning. We begin to fill in what we mean by A or ~A with inquiry. A necessary part of filling in A or ~A is a "universe of discourse" or put more simply, a conversation, embodied place, discipline endowed with empirical examples, etc. The "infinitation of the negative" changes what we mean by "A or ~A," by changing the meaning of the "~" symbol, or returning it to an old meaning. And this changes the logic we find ourselves in. In the case where we believe there is no fact of the matter in a vague situation, that is, if something is genuinely unsettled, so that no investigation will give the "right" answer, there is still a sense in which it is not "A or ~A". Wittgenstein explains how conflicting information arises: from an indefinite, indeterminate situation (a blurred picture). The picture gets blurred as you get further away, or it gets smaller.

This is a law. The fact the blurred details of pictures, sight, or measurements give rise to conflicting information is the fact that links vagueness to logical pluralism, in the context of inquiring with the senses. Conflicting information is unavoidable, when looking at details that are borderline too small for the measurement, A and ~A is one logical way to begin describing this vague situation. And there are numerous logical ways (classical, paraconsistent) of dealing with this situation.

In a sense, because of vagueness no logic is perfectly adequate. A totalitarian would say as soon as we acknowledge more than one logic, we have no logic at all. However certain situations lend themselves to one logic or another. At times, we have such a clear, "universal" picture of the situation (because it must both be clear and be unable to be made unclear, e.g. distinct), that the vagueness can be completely ignored, at times pretending we have a "universal" picture, even though we do not, helps persuade people to our side. The rhetorical use of logic is not a good or bad thing in itself. If we are talking about constructions, constructive logic works best. If the picture is blurred in any relevant way, probability or paraconsistent logic is more appropriate. If the picture is blurred in irrelevant ways, relevant logic is available. Just because we have a clear picture sometimes, doesn't mean we should ignore vague situations, or wish they would go away. Vagueness will not go away.

Classical logic may have arisen as the logic independent of experience because it is the logic with the least amount of vagueness allowed. "All the calculi in mathematics have been invented to suit experience and then made independent of experience." (p43 Wittgenstein 1976) But if vagueness is granted as a law of physics, then how is it that classical logic rose from experience, given that vagueness sits opposite to logic? Dewey believed that logic rose out of experience, but that is a very different view from what came before in the west. Awareness of vagueness, and the invention of logic to try to understand this awareness, is bound in the same activity—inquiry.

In vague situations, logics that are designed to handle conflicting or tentative information are actually more precise than classical logic, they are further along in the investigation, not just at the beginning with "A or ~A". Other logics require that some inquiry has already begun, so that we can choose our logic based on empirical evidence. All logics are abstracted from experience. The question that gives rise to logical pluralism is "Which experience?" Vagueness troubles classical logic, and forces it to face experience, not be independent of it.

Probability theory gives another way of dealing with vague situations, so that the assertion of A and ~A are given real-valued degrees. Still, this does not completely solve vagueness because a real-valued degree can also suffer from vagueness. Significant figures are an example of this—the real number has a certain precision, go beyond that precision and you are in vague territory. This comes into play any time real numbers are applied for real measurements, anytime one uses real numbers in empirical inquiry.

> One serious objection ...is that it really replaces vagueness with the most refined and incredible precision. Set membership, as viewed by the degrees of truth theorist, comes in precise degrees, ... The result is a commitment to precise dividing lines that is not only unbelievable but also thoroughly contrary to what I [call] "robust" or "resilient" vagueness. For ... it seems an essential part of the resilient vagueness of ordinary terms such as "bald", "tall", and "overweight" that in Sorites sequences ... there is indeterminacy with respect to the division between the conditionals that have the value 1, and those that have the next highest value, whatever it might be. It is this central feature of vagueness which the degrees of truth approach, in its standard form, fails to accommodate, regardless of how many truth-values it introduces'. " (Tye 1994, p 14)

A real-truth-value creates uncountably many precise boundaries (if vagueness does not enter into the continuum), but this is the opposite assertion to the basic problem of vagueness—that there are situations with no clear boundary. Adding precise boundaries (arbitrarily) cannot solve the problem of there being no precise boundary, except arbitrarily.

Probability theory depends on real numbers and is only a partial solution to the vagueness that results in logical pluralism, because

> ...probability theory might provide a canon for evaluating degrees of belief, ... Nonetheless, probability theory cannot be a complete answer here, for we also make assertions and denials (and hypotheses and many other things besides), and these may also be evaluated for coherence, using the norms of deductive logic. In particular, we hold that it is a mistake to assert the premises of a valid argument while denying the conclusion... (Beall & Restall 2006, loc 292)

At the same time, inquiry that is not settled, that constructions build towards answering in the future, could be seen as a kind of vagueness, as Rowland (2000) asserts that the question itself is an expression of vagueness.

We can begin to see how probability theory, constructive logic, and paraconsistent logic entwine. Another way to see how they are related is in looking at their definitions of negation. The principle of contradiction (nowadays is formulated as "~~A —> A") is important because Peirce claims that when the principle fails we are in a vague situation. The principle depends on the classical negation operation. The law of contradiction is not true in constructive logic, and negation is different. As will be shown in the Logic Puzzle innovation, a paraconsistent logic has a different way of calculating with the negation symbol. For probability theory the negation of a probability A is the complement: 1-A. Dewey offers an old version of negation that blows up to infinity.

In particular, vagueness troubles the idea that we can make things precise indefinitely: the "..." or induction. Induction is the idea that after a certain number of measurements, we can generalize to say that we will always get about the same measurement, that we know the measurement. This is the movement from experiment to theory generation. Under this definition we may call numbers with an indefinite decimal expansion a theory. ""Surely you can see we needn't go on"—all I know is that you won't go on. If you leave off dividing and do something else instead, what is it that you have shown? Now Watson said we believe that copying this will do. Will do for what? What trick is it supposed to do?" (Wittgenstein 1976, p125) The "trick" is induction. Empirically, numbers with infinite decimal expansion succumb to vagueness. As we become more precise we lose sight of any meaningful sense of size. The calculations seem definite, but the meaning of our calculation has changed to become uncertain, indeterminate, vague.

Constructive logic offers an alternative definition of real numbers. (Bishop 1967) The deep insight that the classical Law of Excluded Middle asserts that all questions "in reality" are already settled (Brouwer 1981) is the reason constructive logic rejects the Law of Excluded Middle. In classical analysis, real numbers, with the axiom of completeness, assert that reality is "finished" and vagueness is an illusion pasted over the ordered field of real numbers. The view that vagueness is real, and is the incarnation of inquiry is expressed here. Asserting that vagueness is not an illusion calls the current formulation of the real numbers into question.

Vagueness has a mathematical reality in the same sense that other mathematical objects are offered as real, and similar to the physical phenomena we encounter. We encounter vagueness because our logical rules along with our observations agree that borderlines are not clear. Vagueness is apparent to the naked eye, but it is traditionally opposed to what can be grasped rationally. "In general, Leibniz had followed the other great rationalists in interpreting perception as a confused form of thinking. Like Descartes, he had treated the deliverances of the senses as sometimes clear but never distinct."(Walsh; Edwards Ed. 1972, p 307) However, vagueness is a clear and distinct concept, and it seems that it also is in complete agreement with the "deliverances of the senses." Thus, in the sense of mathematics that Whewell and others held, vagueness is a truly mathematical one, that is, "…in mathematics there was no difference between objective reality and subjective knowledge; the human mind was completely in tune with external fact." (Richards 1980, p 362) Rational thought and empirical observation are brought together into one concept: vagueness.

Peirce has made some enigmatic comments about vagueness, including the claim:

> I have worked out the logic of vagueness with something like completeness, but need not inflict more of it upon you, at present." (Peirce 1960, p 506)

Although the paper on this "logic of vagueness" is either lost or never done. I propose logical pluralism as the logic of vagueness. This is how vagueness and logical pluralism intertwine in inquiry. Dewey's view that logic is the result of inquiry is adopted here, and the point is that because our inquiry leads us into empirical investigation that is necessarily vague, other logics begin to crop up and we begin to see how one is more appropriate than another given the type of inquiry or situation.

Setting up the empirical problem to be solved

3.1 How do students respond to learning about vagueness?

As a logic teacher in Thailand, I can attest to a confusion reached by the students that Classical logic is the "right" way to think. Classical logic is usually taught to M4-5 students in Thailand. The problem is exacerbated by the vague terminology in the Thai Official Curriculum, which requires students to show "Suitable reasoning" without supplying a hint as to what suitable reasoning is. Teachers and the curriculum have an expectation of Thai students, that of "suitable reasoning" (Thai Standard M6.1), but only the classical logic course normally given to Thai students (and the probability course) lets students know what is meant by this expectation that teachers have. Is this intentional?

Understanding vagueness is key for students to understand the vague curriculum requirement "suitable reasoning". It may be that the requirement is left vague on purpose so as not to require students to think in a particular way, and logical pluralism, a response to vagueness, does not endanger students' freedom to think how they wish, it merely gives students options, without closing off the possibility of inventing new options.

Why isn't vagueness a focus of study in grade school? (or perhaps not vagueness directly, but situations that border on two theories/phenomena) Vagueness is a highly general and pervasive question. This study must leave the problem of vagueness partially undealt with and become more focused. To situate and limit vagueness, the study focuses on how young students respond to a scientific experiment about a vague situation, and an innovation that may help study the effects of logical pluralism is offered up. The relationship between vagueness and logical pluralism as parts of inquiry, explored as a theoretical contribution above, is not focused upon in the empirical study.

3.1.1 Significance of solving this problem

Sprod (2017) argued that teaching science involved dealing with overly precise concepts in the less precise situation of a classroom. Vagueness could act as a kind of bridge between these two linguistic situations. It is hoped that a theory about how students respond to witnessing vagueness will emerge using grounded theory on classroom transcripts, worksheets and interviews.

Another problem at hand is how to bring a difficult topic, logical pluralism, to a wide audience online. This has been done before with the calculus and many other topics. Most topics taught to young students and the general public were at one time at the forefront of research. Somehow these topics were simplified and made available to some extent. The web app purported to do this is available online at http://159.89.203.232/LogicPuzzleDataCollection-Dev/. It is expected that the app will be studied, but not within the scope of this dissertation.

Use of vague language has been developing for these students since primary school (Rowland 2000). Exploring how students respond to an encounter with vagueness can guide the overall project of making logical pluralism available, since vagueness is both immediately available to the senses, and a deep philosophical and mathematical problem that motivates using different logics.

3.1.2 Embedding vagueness and logical pluralism into curriculum

Lipman created his curriculum for the full range of pre-college ages. He argued that "ambiguity" can be taught as early as age 7 (Lipman, Sharp 1980 Loc 816). Even though vagueness is often considered different from ambiguity, P4 students are deemed ready to look at vagueness in my interpretation of the P4C curriculum. Logical pluralism and vagueness problematize the adoption of just one logic, and it is argued in Gazzard that this problematization, or problem-finding, should happen throughout pre-college science classes.

3.2 Philosophy for Children (P4C)

Exploring logical pluralism with the web app online is intended as an emancipating activity. Knowing multiple logics may give students other options for evaluating propositions, emancipating students from having only one (explicit) way. Believing in just one logic (classical logic), and the tandem belief that any illogical thought is beneath reproach—that it is not even worth evaluating—would severely restrict a persons thinking.

This study operates under the tradition called P4C (Philosophy for Children) or Pw(with)C (a movement in education for allowing children to philosophize) in order to bring the student and teacher to the same level when in philosophical dialogue. Studies in the use and abuse of power in the classroom in the context of PwC informs this study, as logical pluralism is intended to be an emancipatory subject. "This is to suggest that the discursive form that characterizes philosophy for children— communal dialogue in an ideal speech situation—is inherently subversive of the goals of biopower, and as such represents a sort of Trojan Horse wheeled into the ideological state apparatus of Western schooling." (Vansieleghem, Kennedy 2012, p. 10).

PwC was founded in pragmatism, but has disavowed those roots when necessary. Lipman, the founder of P4C, was heavily influenced by Dewey and pragmatism.

> Philosophy for Children offers a distinctive perspective in a number of key areas of inquiry and provides a counter-narrative to psychological and sociological perspectives that often dominate educational discourse. Its radical move, in bringing child and philosophy together, has made a unique contribution to the blurring of disciplinary boundaries and opened up new avenues for scholarly inquiry. P4C is a field in its own right through its articulation of philosophy in, rather than of education. (Gregory et al 2017, p xxii).

Sharp (1995), Slade (1997), and Nussbaum (2010) admit that the P4C movement must include other perspectives besides pragmatics and western philosophy.

> I'll give you three reasons. One is… we need radical
> alternatives to be shocked out of our habitual ways of
> seeing…and also sometimes just to re-discover the
> meaning of our own ways. Second, if philosophy is a
> way of life, as many of us here believe, then these
> alternatives are actually 'existential options', in
> Hadot's sense.53 And third, we have to do our best to
> sympathize with options we don't take ourselves, in
> order to avoid violent conflict and to become citizens
> of the world." (Gregory, ed. Vansieleghem & Kennedy
> 2012, pp. 42-43).

The promoting an awareness of the plurality of thinking, being
aware of and accepting vagueness as the reason we need this
plurality of thinking, is part of a path to becoming "citizens of
the world".

The theme of liberation, from domination by the powerful,
is also strongly present in the literature of P4C. "But philosophy
has always been culturally critical and even subversive, going
back to Socrates. Think of Nietzsche's call to do philosophy with
a hammer. Think of Jane Addams' work in Hull House. And this
element has been emphasized by many of our colleagues, who see
P4C as a way of getting children, not merely to think critically,
but to be critical of the world." (Gregory, ed. Vansieleghem &
Kennedy 2012, p. 35). See e.g. Morehouse, 1994; Vigliante,
2006; and Sharp, 2009.

Is learning logical pluralism liberating? "critical
theorists…suspect that rationality itself is a practice of
domination…The part of critical theory that points to a more
enlightened society or a more self-determined human subject is
in tension with the part that sees rational autonomy as a liberal
contrivance." (Gregory, ed. Vansieleghem & Kennedy 2012, p.
36). How to describe "a more enlightened society" without some
kind of rationality? Logical pluralism is about human rationality,
but gives no single answer. Pragmatics cannot answer this
question, because choosing a logic "for now" is not merely a
useful option but an "existential option." The logic chosen carries
with it important philosophical assumptions.

Pragmatics, however, is part of the discussion, and the fact that different logics bring clear and distinct usefulness to a given situation adds urgency to the 'existential options' in logics. Logical pluralism is a rational topic, even if the boundaries between each logic are deep spaces of irrationality. Logical monism is indeed a practice of domination. As Ernest says at the end of his book,

> "In his Ethics of Geometry, Lachterman (1989, back cover), quotes Salomon Maimon's emblematic dictum: "In mathematical construction we are, as it were, gods." I have argued that in the social construction of mathematics we act as gods in bringing the world of mathematics into existence. Thus mathematics can be understood to be about power, compulsion, and regulation."(Ernest 1998, p 276)

3.3 The Stimuli

3.3.1 The Light Box

There are two empirical studies (Sprod 1994, Ferriera 2012), to my knowledge, that offer physics investigations as a tool or medium for teaching the interaction between science and Philosophy for Children (P4C). P4C begins with a stimulus (usually reading) and then moves into what is called a Community of Inquiry (CoI). The CoI is a group discussion where the students choose the question to be discussed. In neither of these published studies is developing physical stimuli a focus. Sprod (1994) studied whole class discussion in the tradition of P4C to see if the quality of discussion could develop while discussing scientific topics. He found a significant increase in scientific reasoning in the P4C class as compared to a control group and qualitatively confirmed that the discussion quality improved.

The topics touched on philosophy of science, such as the uncertain nature of induction. There was one physical activity in the course of the experiment, and the resulting discussion led Dr. Sprod (1998) to believe that physical activity was less conducive to quality whole class discussion than the reading stimuli that he used for the other P4C sessions. He believed this was due to the lack of possible interpretations, of possible problems to find, that the physical "experiment" allowed compared to reading.

> "The questions of the strength of the conclusions that can be drawn from inductive reasoning (Lesson 7) and the nature of the variables that must be controlled in testing or the place of visualization and idealization in science (Lesson 17) are more open-ended than the question of what static and current electricity are. They are more philosophical, so the teacher is less constrained by the "right answer." (Sprod 1998, p474)

Yet Gazzard (1993), one of the few to publish on the subject of using P4C in science, argued without empirical evidence that scientific knowledge consists of tentative interpretations of events and data. This makes scientific knowledge open to further interpretation, but Sprod was unwilling or unable to problematize the experiment on static and current electricity. "One cannot hold concepts tentatively if one cannot find problems in them;"(p625 Ibid 1993) Ferriera's study "..aimed at identifying what role the components of a science curriculum modeled on P4C played in the learning of basic science process skills by a class of fifth graders." (Ferriera 2012, p75) Ferriera used both reading and "hands on activities" to stimulate P4C's Community of Inquiry.

The "light box" is a novel physical experiment made to stimulate a community of inquiry in P4C. The intention was to see if discussion easily crosses over from the physical to philosophy. The light box allows exact wavelengths of green, red and blue light to shine on precisely crafted "rough mirrors". This investigation does not require reading, unlike normal P4C.

Figure 3.3.1A (1/2cm by 1/2cm)   Figure 3.3.1B (1cm by 1cm)

Figure 3.3.1C (2cm by 2cm)   Figure 3.3.1D (4cm by 4cm)

The student investigation mimics a scientific experiment. The (light) environment is controlled, so that all that is seen is precise wavelengths of light on the mirrors, and darkness. The mirrors are rough, but they follow a pattern and a progression. One starts with the 4x4cm rough mirror (1D), and progresses to 2x2 (1C), 1x1(1B) and finally 1/2x1/2cm(1A) faces. The half-cube easily seen in 1D progresses to smaller half-cubes that become more indistinct—this is the concept of vagueness. In a normal scientific experiment, like looking at something with a microscope, the point is to see more distinctions and gain a more precise picture of reality.

But if one were to apply a microscope to ever smaller rough mirrors in the pattern shown above, the vagueness or indistinctness would persist no matter how powerful the microscope (assuming a perfect construction of ever-smaller rough mirrors). Vagueness is usually what is dispelled with a microscope, but in this progression of rough mirrors, vagueness is inductively persistent with any magnification, so that vagueness can be said to generalize into a physical property (Russell 1923). With sufficient fervor of belief, one could construct very finely rough mirrors, in the tradition of contriving to take photographs of the molecular structure of substances.

One way you could show that these mirrors reveal conflicting information is to have them count the number of "cubes" or half-cubes at a distance. Everyone will get the number right for 1D (above), there is just one half-cube, but for 1A, different students will probably get conflicting information on how many half-cubes there are.

The principle of contradiction, invented by Aristotle, is the principle that "A is B" and "A is not B" are mutually exclusive. So we could say "the rough mirror 1A is 24 half-cubes" and the "the rough mirror 1A is 23 half-cubes." Because the situation is vague, the law of contradiction cannot be applied to claim that only one of these propositions is true cannot be upheld, for sufficiently small/fine rough mirrors. This is why vagueness is real.

The first aim of using this light box is to show the kids how conflicting information is possible in vague physical (and linguistic and mental) situations. This is what makes logical pluralism possible. The second aim is to develop the stimulus (the discussion guide for the lightbox, the capabilities of logic puzzle). The toolbox of questions encourage the teacher to cautiously use leading questions such as "What colors did you see?", "Did any student see something else?", "Did the 1st student see that too?", "Why/why not?" "Does viewing 1A generate more difference in opinion than 1D?" "Is 1A harder to see than another? Why/why not?" "Is this property, of getting smaller and harder to see, something you find in everyday life?", "Do words have a similar property? Numbers?" "Can anyone think of an example of something that looks like one thing, but as you get closer it looks like two things?"

> "Finding the right balance between being over-directive (and thus killing genuine student inquiry) and too lax (and thus losing any rigour in the discussion) is not always easy, and will come with experience. As the agenda is set by the students and the actual direction of the discussion ought to arise from their enthusiasm, there is still considerable need to to 'think on your feet', especially if they choose to go with a question for which there is no discussion guide." (Sprod 2011, p13)

The community of inquiry is made to handle multiple interpretations (Gazzard 1993). Usually what people think of as unproblematic on their own, becomes problematic when brought to a community of inquiry, because words are interpreted in different ways by different people. The work of the community of inquiry is to try to reconcile and become aware of these various interpretations, even advance to new ones. The light box is not like an ordinary scientific experiment because the purpose is to show that physical phenomena are open to interpretations just like words.

The conflicting information may become a source of questions to be discussed in the community. Ultimately, the light box experiment is not fundamentally different from other scientific experiments, allowing students to perceive that scientific theory in general is interpretation by a community of scientists. With the light box activity, students are initiated into doing their own interpretations of physical phenomena in their own communities.

"Is it even always an advantage to replace an indistinct picture by a sharp one? Isn't the indistinct one often exactly what we need?"' (Wittgenstein 1953 as quoted in Channell 1994, p6) Indeed, the students will see first hand how the more vague the mirror, the more the blue, red, and green light mixes into white. This is an example of how we need vagueness, because without it we would not be able to perceive white objects, because all white surfaces, even smooth ones, act as a very finely rough mirror. This would mean that the "truth" (when red light shines on a white surface, red is visible, etc) that a white surface tells us is the result of extreme vagueness. Now one may argue that a white surface is no longer vague, even if we see the progression from a rough mirror to a white surface. Such an argument depends on not doing the magnification that Frege believes is required to make an investigation scientific. If magnification is applied, the white surface will look more and more like a rough mirror, eventually looking similar to the left-most picture below, for the 4cmx4cm sided mirror.

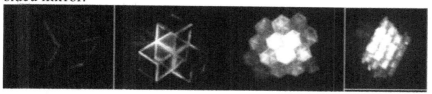

Figure 3.3.1E Rough mirrors inside the light box

The progression is from black to white, but in a sense the only thing that has changed when going from black to white is your perspective on the same thing. This is how something can be both black and white depending on how you look at it, or be both true and false depending on how you look at it. The vague situation between white and black is not just grey, it is an explosion of color and possibility, it in a sense is not determined by its end points/nonvague situations.

> "To paraphrase Raffman [1994: 41 n. 1], it isn't merely that there is tolerance between (determinate) cases of baldness and (determinate) cases of non- baldness. There is tolerance between baldness "and any other category-even a `borderline' category". Or Wright [1976: §11: "no sharp distinction may be drawn between cases where it is definitely correct to apply [a vague] predicate and cases of any other sort"." Shapiro. 2006 Locations 373-375).

3.3.2 Logic Puzzle

Logic Puzzle involves fitting puzzle pieces together to create logical statements, graphing and translating the statements from classical to paraconsistent logic, and a separate constructive logic option.

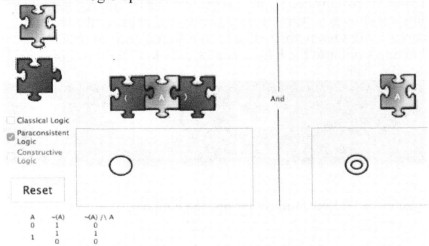

Figure 3.3.2.1

3.3.2.1 Classical Logic
The first thing I want to point out is the circles within circles in the graph part of the picture above. C.S. Peirce invented this notation for classical logic with repeated use of one symbol, the circle. The circle distinguishes between it's inside and outside. It also suggests individuals (A, B, C) by its shape, so ellipses are considered the same symbol as circles. Here is an example

Figure 3.3.2.2
This symbol is equivalent to "~(A AND ~B)", since the outside circle suggests an A on the left, and a ~B on the right of its inside. This symbol is equivalent to "If A, then B". Does it really reduces logic to one symbol, since there are ellipses that suggest "AND"? Shouldn't the assertion be that Peirce's notation reduces logic to the negation and the AND? And to answer I ask, Which is more elemental, the circle/ellipse distinguishing inside and outside or the normal notation for and/not symbols? The fact that space adds together with other spaces in the Peircian graph is an elemental property of space, and requires precisely a lack of notation. Space and its "and" property is where notation, and logical thought, takes place.

For sticklers, there are a few details that should be addressed, first is how do we know which proposition is in which circle? If we make circles from left to right and assume we start with A and proceed to B, etc is that enough? What if we don't know a fact about A but want to talk about B? One way to handle this is to make a convention for writing "A or ~A", then we can say what we like about B. One such convention is to make the circles for "A" and the circle for "~A" touch, so we know that the second circle is not about B but about A. Then we are free to unambiguously talk about B."

For a more interesting detail, one may object that there is really more than one symbol here because there are different circles and ellipses. However we may replace the ellipse/circle symbol with vertical marks all the same. What matters is not the precise geometrical definition of the symbol, but the fact that it distinguishes inside from outside. The same effect could be done with a simple line-mark distinguishing right from left. The mark required for the spirit of the Peircian graph is so elemental it is almost simply the requirement that any mark be written. So:

! | ||

Can be the same symbol as the Peircian circles above, the first and last mark begins and ends the outer ellipse, and the middle two marks are "~B". Putting the last two lines as close together as possible makes the meaning of this notation more or less unambiguous. However, all notation is ambiguous, including classical logic notation:

> "Now imagine we had written down ten thousand ~'s[~ is the negation symbol, ~~A = A]. (You couldn't imagine this. But suppose you saw the whole floor covered; or the road from here to Trumpington.) Now is this one of Russell's formulae? How do you know which formula it is? We might say, "If a man counts them correctly—if he does not make a mistake—he will know." But what is a 'mistake' here?"(Wittgenstein 1976, p273)

However, it seems that "space" in Peirce's logic graphs is the "AND" operator, which is contrary to the idea that space is Difference (see Plato's Sophist for the claim that space is Difference, or a "not-being" that separates/distinguishes beings). Space is, rather, the place where objects are arrayed together; space is not the marker of difference, but the site for likeness. All it takes is to put conflicting Peircian graphs next to each other to see that this space is irrational, non-euclidean and with no metric.

The monstrous quality that runs through Borges's enumeration consists, on the contrary, in the fact that the common ground on which such meetings are possible has itself been destroyed. What is impossible is not the propinquity of the things listed, but the very site on which their propinquity would be possible. The animals "(i) frenzied, (j) innumerable, (k) drawn with a very fine camelhair brush"- where could they ever meet, except in the immaterial sound of the voice pronouncing their enumeration, or on the page transcribing it? Where else could they be juxtaposed except in the non-place of language? Yet, though language can spread them before us, it can do so only in an unthinkable space. The central category of animals "included in the present classification", with its explicit reference to paradoxes we are familiar with, is indication enough that we shall never succeed in defining a stable relation of contained to container between each of these categories and that which includes them all:.. Absurdity destroys the and of the enumeration by making impossible the in where the things enumerated would be divided up. Borges ... does away with the site, the mute ground upon which it is possible for entities to be juxtaposed...What has been removed, in short, is the famous 'operating table'...the table upon which, since the beginning of time, language has intersected space." (Foucault 1973, pg xvi-xvii)

It appears that Peirce's graphs propose to mend this rupture between "language" and "space", because the space in the graph joins the propositions together, no matter whether one proposition is "The animals are frenzied" and another is "The animals are innumerable". And the space in which these things are joined is of symbolic and logical importance.

3.3.2.2 Paraconsistent Logic

A paraconsistent truth table is visible at the bottom of the picture (above). It was drawn because the two statements built are "A" on one side and "~A" on another side. This forces us to leave classical logic and enter paraconsistent logic because paraconsistent logic would allow that A and ~A has a sense in which it is true, while classical logic would explode. The reason for this is entirely based on the difference in negation for each logic. C1 (the paraconsistent logic used in the logic puzzle, invented by Da Costa 1977) creates a new row in the truth-table, effectively creating two senses for when a true possibility is negated, one in which the negation is true, another in which the negation is false.

How can negation and affirmation(assertion) both exist at the same time? Dewey argues that "the taking of food by an animal is prior to or after rejection of other materials as nonfood. Acts which at one and the same time accept for use and shut out are not sequential. (Dewey 1938 Loc 3196-3200) The connection between organic selection-rejection and logical affirmation-negation is, moreover, a special case of a general principle already laid down. The organic function provides the existential basis of the logical." (Dewey 1938, Loc 3200-3202). If negative propositions are ruled out of the logical domain, comparison must go too. In short, negation is other than mere omission or dropping out of certain considerations, factual and ideational. Some facts and some meanings have to be actively eliminated because they are obstacles that stand in the way of resolution of an unsettled situation. (Dewey 1938, Loc 3223-3225)

The point is that how you handle negation changes how vagueness is handled (or not handled). A difference in negation also gives rise to an entirely different logic. Vagueness, by making the law of contradiction fail, makes the distinction between A: "B is C" and ~A: "B is not C" fail, or it synthesizes them, allowing them an existence in the same space. It is perhaps seen more clearly by using Russel's observation that vagueness is the contrary of precision. The basic distinction is the distinction between "A" and "~A", which shows the relationship between distinction and negation. Since no logic "solves" vagueness completely, a different negation fails in different ways, of eliminating similarity, directing us to continue looking for more kinds of negation, for more logics. This is the mathematical relationship between vagueness and logical pluralism.

> "..he always knows what to do. Except in the case of "Bring me a book and don't bring me a book. We have taught him a technique. He hasn't been provided with any rules in this case ...in giving a contradictory order, I may have wanted to produce a certain effect--to make you gape,... or to paralyze you. One might say, "Well, if this is the effect you wanted, then it does work." (Wittgenstein 1976, p175)

> "Lewy: One might say that an entirely new meaning has been given to the contradiction.
> Wittgenstein: Yes, one might say that.—and notice that contradictions are actually often used in this way. For instance, we say "Well it is fine and it's not fine", meaning that the weather is mediocre. And one might even introduce this use into mathematics."
> (Wittgenstein 1976, p176)

2.8.2.3 Constructive Logic

Vagueness is defined as when the law of contradiction does not hold. Interestingly, for constructive logic the law of contradiction also does not hold. This is because there are different values attributed to a proposition or more accurately a construction, not true/false, but "constructed" (A) "not constructed (and constructable)" ($\sim\sim$A) and "not constructable" ($\sim$A). If something is "not-not constructable," that does not mean that the thing is constructed (to use the modern definition of the law of contradiction, $\sim\sim$A $\rightarrow$ A) Vagueness as the failure of the law of contradiction is not quite enough to get constructive logic, because implication is quirky and specific to constructions. Implication has been a topic of debate even for classical logic. Constructive logic adopts one Stoic version of classical logic implication, but made specific to constructions, that being the version of implication that makes the consequent (the second term in A $\rightarrow$ B) contained in the antecedent (the first), so in constructive logic A $\rightarrow$ B is true when if A is constructed B is also constructed (accidentally). By constructing A, B automatically is already constructed, this is A $\rightarrow$ B. Also the value "constructed" isn't enough, one needs an algorithm for construction of A as proof that it is constructable, or one needs to actually construct A before one can assert "A" in constructive logic. The law of contradiction fails, though, so by definition, constructive logic is vague. In a sense the logic puzzle has a law of excluded middle-like law that A or $\sim$A or $\sim\sim$A. I think this points more to the unsatisfactory definition of vagueness, rather than a fault of constructive logic. In a sense differentiating $\sim\sim$A from A makes constructive logic more precise. One can see how vagueness and precision contaminate each other. It should not come as a surprise that real numbers, an expression of ultimate precision, also creates ultimate vagueness is the pragmatic use of our words. But this is a minor point against an otherwise very useful definition of vagueness.

3.4 The movement between science and philosophy

> One noticeable difference in our scientific community of inquiry from those I was used to in the classroom was the frequency of recourse to spur-of-the- moment experiments suggested and often carried out by the students - a not unexpected response to the differences between scientific and philosophical contexts. Nevertheless, much of the discussion was recognizably philosophical rather than merely empirically scientific."(Sprod 1997, p 11-12)

Is it possible to move back and forth between the scientific and the philosophical, having each movement contribute to the inquiry at hand?

The claim that science is hard to understand because "normal" experience creates a barrier to understanding the results of "abnormal" scientific experiments (Na, Song 2014, p 1032) It seems philosophy suffers from the same problem. We begin with something on the surface, an everyday word or concept, an everyday physical experience, and inquiry draws us away from the common encounter. The fact that we began with the "real-world" adds urgency to our inquiry, even though we quickly leave the "real-world" behind.

> Along these lines, Lipman (1988, chap. 7) highlights that most of the cognitive skills needed in the science classroom are not different from the ones P4C teaches. Although such considerations offer a window into the contribution of P4C to the improvement of science education, they are of a theoretical nature and there is an almost total absence of empirical research conducted on the matter, with the exception of one study (Sprod, 1994)." (Ferreira 2012, p73)

Troubling concepts, finding their fuzzy edges and discussing, building on one another in a community of inquiry is one way, contrived though it may seem, of leaving what began as "the real world." Another way is an equally, if not more so, contrived scientific experiment designed to show something very specific about reality, removed from common "real world" experience. The light box seems to take the form of such a contrivance. The environment in the lightbox is controlled, the experiment is precise, but the antecedent to the experiment is to watch vagueness increase, resolving the colored lights into white. Getting "white" is an important result, even though in a sense it is more vague than where we started (in another sense we have traversed the vague borderline from one clear situation to another). Scientific experiments are not different from philosophical communities of inquiry in that resolutions can be reached when exploring and troubling concepts by expanding vagueness.

Vagueness marries the conceptual work of the community of inquiry and the physical work of science nicely, if there is no fact of the matter whether a particular vagueness is verbal or objective. This can be seen by investigating the concept of vagueness by itself: The vagueness between, say, "high up" and "not high up", (this can easily be pictured on a cartesian graph with a line gradually going down from left to right (Weber 2010)) could be dealt with by adding and third "uncertain" value/region. And the trouble here is, as is well known, that adding a region uncertain only adds two new borderline cases between "high up" and "uncertain", and another borderline case between "uncertain" and "not-high up", so that new "higher order vagueness" is created for these borderline cases. New regions can be created for these new borderline cases, creating more borderlines between regions, and vagueness at borderlines, etc. Ultimately the pursuit of conquering higher-order vagueness by exchanging borderlines(points) with intervals(stuff/extension) is a vagueness between points and intervals.

Moreover, a vagueness between points and intervals is a general problem reproducible anytime vagueness rears its ugly head. If we draw the connections from points to formulae (such as definitions) and from intervals to the substance of formulae, (the formula of an interval is the two endpoints, the substance is the "stuff" between the endpoints) we find that the line between words (their definition) and objects ("stuff") is vague, which is also well known. What is new here is that we found this well known vagueness by investigating vagueness itself in a general way.

> An unanticipated result of the study was the suggestion that triggers based on stories may be more effective in encouraging student reasoning about science than those based on 'surprising' experiments2." (Sprod 1997b, as quoted in Moriyon 2012, p94)

We choose the surprising experiment because it falls outside the periphery of what we understand, and we choose to render concepts "fuzzy" for the same reason. We are encouraging students to "look around," to become aware that things aren't what they seem sometimes. This does not necessarily mean "look closer." The point is the surprising experiment is surprising because of an understanding, an expectation that might as well be conceptual, and also might as well be physical, because this expectation governs and filters how students interact and experience physically with the world. From a very physical perspective, philosophy and science are unified by this search for surprising experiments and fuzzy concepts.

Sprod found that P4C can contribute a significant gain in scientific reasoning. (Sprod 1994, 1997a, 1997b, 1998). However, Ferriera finds a specific challenge to the application of P4C, which is normally conceptual work, to science learning. This poses a challenge for applying P4C pedagogy to the sciences, where observing and manipulating objects (either natural ones or artifacts) are at the heart of the learning experience. (Ferriera 2012, p75)

Ferriera's response to this challenge is to use both hands-on activities and reading as the stimuli for the community of inquiry. Haynes and Murris (2011) also contend that philosophy is usually viewed as something that is purely "abstract or symbolic" (p 3841). Ferriera adds that her study used the technical terminology of science in the readings, unlike normal P4C. This is how science removes itself from everyday experience, similar to philosophies "abstracting" from everyday experience. Here the light-box can contribute because it challenges the need for technical terminology in the science-P4C approach. Vague terms (like big ideas such as "happiness") can still be useful in learning science, because physical phenomena are vague.

3.5 Objectives
main objectives of empirical study:
1. To develop two learning activities toward benefits and away from detriments.
2. To study the light box learning activity (all instruments are studied comparatively between the two cycles of action research) (all instruments: attitude, test performance, classroom transcripts/worksheets, and guided interview)
3. Does learning vagueness make students happy? (including a positive attitude towards mathematics and philosophy) (Attitudinal questionnaires (2)),
4. How are the contents of the course incorporated into the student's life? (Guided Interview)
5. Do students progress from physical/mechanical considerations to philosophical discussion on the concepts contained in these physical/mechanical stimulus (e.g. vagueness and logical pluralism) and if so, how? Is it different from reading stimulus?

To address the main objectives, the attitudinal questionnaire gathers data on a more specific topic than general (or vague) happiness, trying to gauge if students' attitudes toward math and philosophy increase in positivity. The guided interview adds a more longitudinal dimension to the study, with the goal to understand how knowledge of vagueness "happens" to students outside the classroom presentations.

It is hoped that P4C will be found to be the most appropriate method for teaching vagueness. Grounded theory will be used on class transcripts,worksheets, and interviews. With guiding questions such as "Where were the "Aha!" moments, or other happy moments, and how can these moments be duplicated?", the theory will guide the next cycle of action research.

3.6 Happiness goal

Is it necessary that indeterminate situations be marked by confusion, obscurity and conflict? "An unsettled situation needs clarification because as it stands it gives no lead or cue to the way in which it may be resolved. We do not know, as we say, where to turn; we grope and fumble. We escape from this muddled condition only by turning to other situations and searching them for a cue." (Dewey 1938, Loc 3178-3181)

A goal of happiness creates a lot of problems for research. Groping and fumbling for a way to make the research easier: replacing the goal of happiness for our students with the goal "positive attitude towards math" would be enough. However it is the author's belief that it is imperative that these problems be addressed, and happiness be kept as a goal. Doesn't it seem like, faced with the choice between being more sure about the effects of the study ("positive attitude towards math"), or doing for the students something more worthwhile ("happiness"), we choose the more pessimistic, more pragmatic one?

> To erect a philosophical edifice that shall outlast the vicissitudes of time, my care must be, not so much to set each brick with nicest accuracy, as to lay the foundations deep and massive. Aristotle built upon a few deliberately chosen concepts—such as matter and form, act and power—very broad, and in their outlines vague and rough, but solid, unshakable, and not easily undermined." Peirce 1960 CP 1.1

Concentrating on vagueness has another "effect" besides frustrating our attempts of knowing. At the end of each day striving to know things, I return to my household affairs, leaving off technical language for common, unprobing talk with family and the familiar. In this environment I find rest.

It may be argued that I would not find rest if someone hadn't strove for house building techniques, and countless other comforts at home. The human family has been following Peirce's philosophy—that we should look to the effects of our labor (such as happiness) to give meaning to our labor. In the face of all that I benefit from, that gives meaning to my working ancestors, I point out the annoying truth of how little we really know in mathematics, of the "house" built by our ancestors in which we live. Why?

Some of us follow the social tendency to ignore our environment failing us in our project of the Enlightenment. It is not just the environment though, our knowledge has become so powerful, creations so ingenious, that we could destroy ourselves any minute with its power in the form of nuclear war, with hardly more than a thought. There are many other global crises that are hard to recognize when put to the task of giving meaning to our immediate labors.

In Peirce's "house", the key concepts are uses and effects, means and consequences. If we want happiness, then we should do the things that cause happiness. If we want freedom, then get to work on that. The logic of that statement is not just in the form of the if, then. Peirce is making the fundamental concept the "If, then." For all thought, if we want to think about how (the "if") to create desired effects ("then"), then our thoughts should take this form. By nesting If, then within another If, then, the "If, then" of pragmatism becomes hard to undermine, and calls us to work, to act in order to create the desired effects.

Work is another ultimate concept in pragmatism, and pragmatism was born of the natural sciences. Where can we turn to call for rest? We must turn to each other, but not as helpers, not as workers, but with uncertainty. If we turn to each other with judgements: "Anti-vaxxers are bad" we will only alienate each other. That is the effect of having various specialized languages. If, then is a form of analysis, from the container to the (strictly) contained. It analyzes language, refines and specializes language into languages. The certainty we gain from this language separates us from the certainty of another who speaks a different language.

A basic assumption for Peirce and science is that doubt is an uneasy feeling. Vagueness must remain a bad thing because it creates uncertainty. It must be stamped out and struggled against at every turn. I am not going to argue that vagueness is good, although the skeptics believed in Ataraxia, a sense of peace that comes from accepting uncertainty. A peace that is very similar to the peace one feels at the end of the day when specialized knowledge gives way to vague conversation and the less precise arts of cooking dinner and doing the dishes.

I will argue that vagueness can help us, how? It seems as though all it would do is confuse us. An obvious response, from a global point of view, is that we should be totally bewildered. It would seem as though now, especially, we should not be rebelling against the only things that make sense—our sources of meaning and sense of place in the world, our work.

> The same [newspaper] article mixes together chemical reactions and political reactions. A single thread links the most esoteric sciences and the most sordid politics, the most distant sky and some factory in the Lyon suburbs, dangers on a global scale and the impending local elections…The horizons, the stakes, the time frames, the actors—none of these are commensurable, yet there they are, caught up in the same story. (Latour 2002, p 1)

Vagueness (taken as a general concept, even though Peirce would never allow the two concepts to entwine) offers a connection between specialized language and common "lived" language, because specialized knowledge succumbs to vagueness just as much as we do in the ordinary parts of our daily lives. If we become comfortable with vagueness, we can begin to allow the Lyon suburbs and the distant sky to be the factory nearby, and the sky above us. Vagueness opens up the possibility of interpretation, so that the newspaper article's interpretation doesn't have to be our own.

I only want to argue that we should pay attention to vagueness. Not in an uneasy or struggling way but in an ordinary matter-of-fact way. Vagueness is there, it is everywhere; it is real; it is a fact. Without it we could assert nothing in words or symbols. Acknowledging it and giving it importance does no harm, and makes us aware of our conditioning that we should be uneasy when we face vagueness.

> We most naturally compare a contradiction to something which jams. I would say that anything which we give and conceive to be an explanation of why a contradiction does not work is just another way of saying that we do not want it to work." (Wittgenstein 1976, p187)

Vagueness allows contradictions, a kind of "jamming" in the epistemological works. The idea that vagueness is always at the limits of our knowledge implies that we are constantly in a jam. We defer this jamming to future work tomorrow. And so we subsist on the past (our house) and the future. It can not be emphasized enough that the world we live in now would benefit more, would have a more desirable effect, if all of us did less work. Certainly the kinds of work should change towards things like social work, but also quite a bit less work is needed. This truth seems to betray our human heritage. If we give up pushing the boundaries of our knowledge, we leave the entire edifice just as jammed as it was when we began. Even though it jams our epistemological systems, it also creates a kind of freedom that we need for decent survival.

And that freedom can be found in logical pluralism, where alternatives to Peirce's philosophy of the "if, then" are found, indeed, proven to exist by Peirce's own definition of vagueness, where he alludes to a "logic of vagueness." However, these "logics of vagueness" are not importantly progressive. One can progress in one logic, but the main focus is on plurality, on understanding "other" logics. The motivation changes from how, which searches for a (the one most efficient) technique, an "if" in classical logic, to when, where, what, who, and why. All these questions come to bear on choosing which logic to use. All this possibility of other logics, in answer to Peirce's all encompassing classical "If, then", is brought with the acknowledgement of vagueness.

When we pay attention to vagueness we can see that the "jam" between Godel's "completeness and consistency" between "A and ~A" is the same as needing our dinner to be hot and our drink to be cold, of the lightness and mass of our breath, of the words we say in casual conversation and the unsaid words of love we mean.

When we do this, we move closer to human happiness, which is more important than progressive use or effects or work, and ultimately happiness is not the effect of building a house or cooking dinner. Yes happiness comes from within, it also comes from each other. It is claimed that work is how one pursues happiness.

> But humans are a special kind of creature, who share, through communication, a common aim: (as Aristotle put it) 'eudaimonia', or flourishing, if not happiness. Granted, we all conceive this aim in slightly different ways, but few of us imagine that it is more likely to be achieved by fighting against each other than by working with each other." (Sutcliffe 2014, p34)

However, I would claim that happiness comes before work, since we always succumb to vagueness, returning from our specialized or concentrated states of work to the vague existence of home and family. Not only do we always succumb to vagueness at the end of the work day, but we were there to begin with. Perhaps this realization can help someone be happy before doing so much work, maybe it will allow more rest.

Methodology

4.1 Nature of mathematics

This study is informed by the social constructivist movement, specifically as a philosophy of mathematics (Ernest, 1998) which is based on a faliblistic view of mathematics, that mathematics is fundamentally an evolving, creative discipline that is corrigible, as opposed to the absolutist view that mathematics grows incrementally but not fundamentally, and is an incorrigible discipline about discovery not creativity. Ernest draws heavily from Lakatos (1976), who puts forward a dialogic, quasi-historical view of mathematical creativity. Classical logic is fallible, as well as any other logic, and teaching this fallibility has a rhetorical effect on the certainty of the rest of mathematics. The study is informed by the so-called 'maverick' tradition in mathematics "In differing ways Davis and Hersh (1980), Kitcher (1984), Lakatos (1976), Tymoczko (1986a), Tiles (1991), Wittgenstein(1956), and others have argued for a critical reexamination of traditional presuppositions about the certainty of mathematical knowledge."(Ernest 1998, p xii) For thousands of years in the west philosophers took mathematics as the fundament of knowledge on which other disciplines are built. The maverick tradition's critical stance towards mathematics has significance for these other disciplines, as well as for whether we can know anything at all.

Vagueness enlivens criticism of mathematical doctrine, which in turn brings other disciplines into doubt. Feyerabend (1999, p 39) noted the "fault lines" or vague borderlines in physics between, say, Newtonian physics and chemical reality, between atomic physics and quantum physics. However, the fault line can be seen as a general epistemic problem, not just a physical problem.

> "By reductionist, I mean the positivist doctrine, much beloved of the Logical Empiricists, that there is an hierarchy of objects, theories or disciplines, and it is possible to translate and replace objects, theories or disciplines further up the hierarchy into the objects, terms, concepts and theories lower down the hierarchy without loss of generality or scientific significance. Thus, according to this scheme, sociology can be translated (reduced) to psychology, psychology to biology, biology to chemistry,
> chemistry to physics, and finally physics to mathematics." (Ernest 2008, p 3)

If vagueness enters between these areas of knowledge, it draws reductionism into question. Ernest goes on:

> "[some scholars] misrepresent such philosophies [constructivism] as saying that mathematics can be reduced to sociology…(that mathematical matters are decided by 'mob rule'). If these critics subscribe to reductionism, which is not uncommon, then the threat is that by 'joining the ends' mathematics is knocked off its pedestal as the foundation of knowledge, and the whole chain of disciplines closes on itself in a viscous circle, knowledge eating itself like the worm Ouroboros." (Ernest 2008, p 7)

If mathematics is to be criticized by pointing to vagueness, then another foundation of knowledge should be offered. Skeptics, while denying that knowledge is possible, still took immediate sense-perception as a ground. The recourse that Rowland (2000) takes as a result of studying the indeterminacy of vagueness in the math classroom is to ground knowledge in pragmatics, in discourse analysis and semiotics, where vagueness is recognized to be useful and have positive effects.

Ernest took dialogue as the ground of mathematical knowledge. For example, the epsilon-delta mathematical definition of continuity (see Abbot 2001, p 109) is widely known to have a dialectic nature (Ernest 1998, p 170),). "Although it is claimed that the dialogical nature of mathematics has been hidden, it is still evidence in a number of ways (Ernest 1994a)." (Ernest 1998, p 168) This definition of continuity conceals its dialectic nature in favor of a deductive-like form. If logical monism is to be strictly adhered to, a great deal of normally accepted thought is excluded, even from mathematics itself.

It must be admitted that my own epistemological foundation is not in social constructivism or pragmatics. My own background, the way I avoid the Oroborous eating my certainty, is with Buddhist doctrines like that of Kamma (action), of ignorance (vagueness) as the root cause of all conditioned things (logically conditioned or otherwise). The ground taken in these classrooms is not dialogue. Informed action, based on the awareness and limitation of vagueness is the ground, and action research is the fundamental research in this empirical study. Immediate sense-perception is a part of this ground, but the ground is extended to the sensory contact between mind and concepts and the act of instructing the teacher to teach students vagueness, to make similar contact to similar (communicated) concepts. In this case of action research in teaching and learning vagueness, the ground is not totally stable, since vagueness and its limits contaminate each other.

4.2 Methodology and Logic

> ...the field indicated, that of inquiries, is already pre-empted. There is, it will be said, a recognized subject which deals with it. That subject is methodology; and there is a well recognized distinction between methodology and logic, the former being an application of the latter." (Dewey 1938 Locations 166-168)

Dewey writes that the reason methodology and logic are seen as separate is logic is needed as an external and certain standard to judge methods of scientific inquiry.

> How can inquiry originate logical forms (as it has been stated that it does) and yet be subject to the requirements of these forms?" (Dewey 1938 Locations 179-180)

> The problem reduced to its lowest terms is whether inquiry can develop in its own ongoing course the logical standards and forms to which further inquiry shall submit. One might reply by saying that it can because it has. One might even challenge the objector to produce a single instance of improvement in scientific methods not produced in and by the self-corrective process of inquiry;" (Dewey 1938 Locations 182-185)

Thus the content of the course, and the (pedagogical) content knowledge to be gained seem more fundamentally concerned with epistemic questions than the research methodology. This study is explicitly critical of probability theory, the basis of statistical hypothesis testing. How does one make assumptions about a methodology when the goal is to be critical of the most fundamental wellsprings of knowledge?

> "Perhaps the single most important skill [of the skills of science learning] for understanding what any hypothesis is doing and for understanding the results of its test, is the ability to think syllogistically. The underlying structure of any hypothesis is "if x, then y."(Gazzard 1993, p627)

The theory presented here is prior to and conditions any "if x, then y" since the if, then depends on which logic you are talking about. The empirical study cannot depend on a totally certain form of "if x, then y." Action research (McNiff 2006) is the most important and basic form of research in this study. It may be that action research is even more fundamental than logical knowledge. Knowledge can be gained by doing, in this case teaching, looking at vagueness, and exploring logical pluralism with Logic Puzzle.

Grounded theory (Glaser & Strauss 1967) is needed because there is no literature on logical pluralism, or the comparison between multiple deductive logics, as a topic of study in education. P4C may be the correct teaching theory for logical pluralism, but that is not assumed, and the correct teaching theory may develop independently of P4C. The Predict/Observe/Explain method is also used for the experiment part, before the CoI. Interviews and class videos, along with worksheets and an online forum discussion will be analyzed to gain an understanding of what students think about this topic and the method of teaching, and how their responses evolve through the course and afterwards. The grounded theory generated from this analysis will inform the next cycle of action research.

The quantitative tests are the most tentative form of research applied in this study. As methods of deduction are explored, it may well be that simple right or wrong questions will be (rightly) questioned and even over-thought. The contents of logical pluralism are expected to change the way students read a normal logic test. The students will require a lot more description of what exactly is asked because the students will have more logical tools than a normal student. The post-test will mainly be to understand if/how the courses improve logic selection in different logic stories.

Nonparametric statistics was used because it is difficult to assume a probability distribution for these samples. Instead, it may be best to investigate nonparametrically whether or not the pre- and post- results have the same probability distribution that is shifted by some unknown amount. This could yield an interesting statistical result without making an assumption about the probability distribution.

4.3 Research design

Action research works in a cycle— it attempts to perfect a process, in this case of teaching and learning multiple logics, by practicing through action, reflecting on what worked, and planning the next action in the next cycle. For this research the first cycle examines the introduction of the rough mirrors in the light box for P4 students, and the encounter with the Logic Puzzle logical pluralism teaching tool, by looking at the class transcript and interview for the P4 students, the worksheets for both, and the discussion (in person for the P4 students, online forum for the Logic Puzzle). Does the intervention contribute to a positive attitude towards mathematics? Data of older (high school and up) people respond is compared to the idea of logical pluralism to the P4 response to vagueness—the concept that makes logical pluralism possible—that some knowledge can be gained about whether pluralism should be the way students are introduced to logic for the first time or not. For both the online group, and the P4 students, a community of inquiry will follow—on an online forum for the online group, and in class for the P4 students. However, proponents of P4C (Lee 2014, p 80) caution that it takes weeks to develop a "community of inquiry" (CoI). The possibility of a CoI was assessed by trying to have a discussion according to the P4C guidelines and seeing what can be done given the limitations of the study (only one one-hour session of CoI). It was found that attempting CoI was impractical, although the data gathered was still interesting, the students were not able to work together as a community of inquiry. As a result, a teacher-focused approach was used in the 2nd cycle.

After the first research intervention, coded data accumulates using grounded theory. Analysis for a pattern began by asking, "How do students respond to the vague encounter?" "Are the students becoming thinking philosophically?" "Are the student's reasoning becoming more developed, more free and flexible, with these hands-on exercises, and if so how?" In the next cycle (there will be two passes of action research), while the light box will stay the same, the discussion guide for the light box evolved, becoming more directed toward the specific question the light box raises: is color, specifically white a result of vagueness, and if so, is color real? The Logic Puzzle evolved based on user feedback.

4.4 Data collection and Analysis

The action research cycle:

1. Apply Intervention to test stimuli and CoI guide and collect data using attitudinal questionnaire, videotape, and worksheets.
2. Analyze data and generate grounded theory by considering data using t-test and grounded theory.
3. Modify next intervention based data, recording the changes.
4. Cycle back to step 1.

4.4.1 Outcome measurement

1. Intensive reading, The researcher will read closely the words of the transcript, being interested in the various possible meanings that each word could have meant, deciding which meanings are reasonable to explore further and coding said meanings.

2. Questioning: The researcher will record any questions that arise during the intensive reading, any anomalous or interesting parts of the data that require more probing to answer

3. Comparisons: After the researcher has coded the data, a comparison between the various codes will take place. The goal is to make the data cohere so a larger theory can form.

4. Flip-flop technique (Corbin & Strauss 2008, p79): the researcher will imagine hypothesizing the opposite of what the data seems to be suggesting, to get an idea the range that the researcher is working in, and the significance of what the data actually seems to be representing.

5. Other techniques are applied such as drawing from personal experience and looking for biases from the researcher and the subjects are applied when they seem relevant.

4.4.2 Statistical Analysis

The attitudinal questionnaire were analyzed for changes in attitude towards mathematics using a 5-point scale from Strongly Agree to Strongly Disagree. 8 of the statements in the attitudinal questionnaire are basic positive or negative attitudes about math. 4 of the statements, are not there to gauge interest in math, but rather are an attempt to study other attitudes about math and how they might change because of learning about vagueness or logical pluralism.

Data and Results

There were many possibilities to expect from the intervention. Which ones were actually present in the exploration of the light box and the discussion? First the statistical results are presented, then a description of what happened follows. Finally there is a discussion of the successes and failures.

5.1 Quantitative results

One statistical result came from measuring the time students took to look at different sized mirrors. The 4x4 mirror was unambiguously dark in the light box. A matched pair t-test between the 4x4cm and 1x1cm look times confirms that the vague situation of the 1x1cm mirror invited more investigation. Figure 5.1.1: Look Times

1st Turn Look Times For Each Student

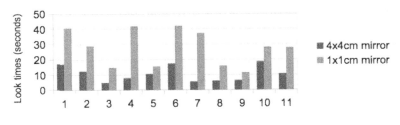

Students (11 is average)

Figure 5.1.1: Look Times

Cohen's D Effect Size: 1.75 (Very Large)

Matched Pair 1-tail t-test p=0.0004

A pre- and post- mathematics attitudinal questionnaire was given. 10 students responded to 8 positive and negative statements on a scale of 5 options from Strongly Agree to Strongly Disagree. Student's attitude toward math improved. (Matched Pair Sign Test, n = 7, p = 0.11)

Three questions had moderate Cohen's D effect size over the 10 students, these were tested using a t-test. One was significant: "Math interests me." (p=0.047, Effect size: 0.41)

A good reason for expecting that the intervention would have a positive effect on students attitudes towards math is 1) that the mirrors are clearly mathematical, with precise measured mirror squares arranged and presented in a mathematical progression from largest to smallest, 2) from an anecdote the teacher had: "teacher observation, kids that usually misbehave and don't pay attention/don't understand were really involved and "into it" They started with this attitude when the teacher told them there is no right or wrong answer. "it made them really want to do it" and 3) The apparent surprise and interest the light box and mirrors produced. However, there was no finding from questionnaire about attitudes towards philosophy, so it can not be claimed that the encounter with vagueness improved attitudes in general.

It is important to wonder at the effect size in the category "Math can describe anything". One may have a reaction to the light box that would have the exact opposite effect, but here we see that acknowledging vagueness, not pretending it is purely philosophical but is part of science and knowledge, has a positive effect on a students attitude towards math. This suggests that, even if it is incorrect to claim vagueness is a mathematical problem, investigating the mathematical progression of rough mirrors increases positivity of attitude towards mathematics.

5.2 Qualitative description

5.2.1 First Cycle

There were prevalent examples of how the vague encounter is difficult to recognize, understand, and describe.

45:54 Hom "I can't remember what I see"
46:03 Teacher "well you can remember as a picture"
student: "Huh? As a picture?"

In the next example, Gus is noticing that what light hits the eye is different at different angles because there is so much light-scattering and reflection. It is clear that there is no right answer for what the students see and write, but they diligently try anyway

> 49:18 Gus "Can we not write down, all I know is that if we change the position/angle of looking, the color change"

Here is another example of vagueness being difficult, but "beautiful" with a twist.

> Hom "The colors look really beautiful but I don't want to write it down"

Why doesn't she want to write it down? Any other reason besides its too hard? Are there situations when writing it down is wrong, or at least misguided?

In the next example, In wants to create a rule such as "As the mirrors get smaller, there is more color" but that rule isn't true which is apparent in the investigation. The reflector has the smallest mirrors but there are fewer colors. The experiment defies theory creation.

> In: "I have question, why less mirror(teacher guesses he means larger faces) we see less light oh on more mirrors have less light. But when more mirrors....
> Kid: "more colors"
> In: " big mirror..(thinking)..color..(thinking)..less mirrors have less colors, more mirrors have more colors??" ...less mirrors, more mirrors...

In the look-time analysis it was apparent that the students want to "look again" and the look times are long in the vague situation. I thought that seeing vagueness would spark questions, but really what it did was create a desire to keep on investigating empirically. I kept asking for questions but really only got two: how to write it down and why the different mirror sizes change what is visible.

1:01:17-1:02 Best "Why when the mirror gets smaller, you see more color, but the reflection thats even smaller, you see less color"

At the end of the the vague encounter the boys theorized about what was going on, they confused the light reflection and light-scattering theories, which is what the experiment does as well; they did not ask questions. But you could say that they had a question in mind that they were trying to answer by inspecting with their eyes and theorizing.

57:51 Bright "theres three colors but they reflect "yeah they come together and mix together" Bright "The light meets/hits (Chongun)"

At the very end of the 1st intervention the students reviewed what they expected a science-learning situation to be, and how this was different from their expectation. The experiment went outside their definition of a science class.

Woon "it's weird not to write a lot when learning Science" 1:03:08 Chennan "when we learn Science, the answer is too easy" ... 1:04:52 Woon "at ...school the teacher was talk, talk and talk, and we write and write. If we didn't finish we wouldn't allow to leave"

There seems to be a few related concepts going on here: difficulty describing vagueness, wanting to experience vagueness first hand, theorizing about vagueness, understanding that when there is no right answer, perspective and subjectivity become very important, the experience of vagueness is not a well-defined activity for the students, that is, they are unfamiliar with this type of science activity. The various concepts are related: because different perspectives matter, it is harder to describe and feel like your description is "really" a description. Because vagueness is harder to describe and harder to experience in a "right answer" way, students want to experience it more, and they want to develop a theory that is the "right answer". Is this really a natural desire (for a right answer) or have they merely gotten used to that kind of teaching? My belief is that vagueness is a "right question" because it is so hard to answer. It crops up in many forms and with so many unsatisfactory answers throughout history.

Imagine a situation where the right answer is clear "the answer is too easy." Sprod had one less philosophical class where the right answer made philosophical discussion harder. He concluded that reading was the best way to make philosophical discussion, but he didn't try using vague physical situations. There are many other ways to explore a vague situation that sits between different (competing?) scientific theories. It may even be that this is where investigation in school should be focused, by watching the students interest in the vague situation, their desire to look, theorize, and their complaints about their "normal" science classes. The reason this type of education is so important is it takes students out of a symbolic representation of the world and allows students to immerse themselves in their own senses. There were examples of students asking philosophical questions (it seems, without realizing they were philosophical):

3:40 Mae Nee: Why when we guess its not the same as when we actually look?

They know that what you see depends on your perspective, but they still don't see what they expect. The idea that they should see what they expect, since what they see depends on their perspective, is interesting but not characteristic of other students or repeated in the data. In the next example it seems students confused the vague situation with the clear one:

> 5:31 Teacher: When the the mirror gets smaller we see more colors right?
> Gus: we see better/more clearly
> Teacher and when it became the reflector how did you see?
> Gus: Then the color is mixing and our eyes can't tell, its mixed very fine and we can't tell what color it is." Teacher: (repeats) eyes can't see, and then what?
> Gus: He sees the normal color
> Teacher: Whats that mean, normal color?
> Gus: Just like the normal color means the light that we started with, and the color is not as many as before.

In the largest mirror there is almost no color, so when he says "before" he means the middle-stages. The smallest stage (reflector) there is also less color than the middle stages. For the middle stages there is an explosion of color, maybe that means you can see better, although what colors one sees is less clear; maybe it makes Gus pay more attention. What did Gus mean by normal? By "Normal" did Gus mean not "real" since the real is revealed in contrived, not normal experiments?

> 26:49 Gus its like saturn
> kid: (about Saturn) its not actually a ring, its particles/rocks

There seems to be a tension between accepting that what they see depends on their perspective, and the idea that you get the "real" by magnification, independent of perspective, the magnified view is "true".

For Saturn, the child used the Thai word "hin" which means rock, but did he confuse this with particles? What the student means works for both rocks and particles, and the confusion reveals why magnifying does not reveal, it only shows another perspective (rocks) that can be further magnified (to particles, etc).

If the situation where reversed, and the lesson of the experiment was that looking closer always yielded truth, would the answer then be "too easy" as the kids described "normal" science? The kids think that saying Saturn's rings aren't real is an interesting thing to say, which suggests that some people don't already know this: that (it is at least commonly believed that) Saturn's rings are real. Speakers often try to seem closer to the truth by quoting a common belief, and then debunking this belief by talking about how things behave at a higher level of magnification, at the level of particles or smaller. Even though this is extremely common, the speaker seems to think they are going against common wisdom and being a "skeptical" scientist instead. The data suggests this common behavior is at play with these 9 year old children.

5.2.2 Second Cycle

The second cycle of action research was guided by the first. This cycle we did both sessions back to back, in one large session. There was no indication that students increased in positive attitude towards math. When the students were discussing the questionnaire they agreed that the experiment was not mathematical. I believe this consensus is why there was no result either way using this instrument. I came away from the first cycle realizing that the students were not understanding that the rough mirrors copy the effect of magnification—that the 2x2 mirror is a 100% magnification of the 1x1 mirror. The students in the first cycle explained away the difficulty of vagueness by saying they could not see closely enough to know what was going on, that they needed magnification.

In the second cycle I tried to make it as clear as I could to the teacher that this point should be addressed and discussed. As such, the cycle was quite different from the first. The first was less directed and more open, the second was directed towards understanding how students can deal with vagueness, knowing that magnification is already available to them (in the form of the larger mirrors), as they grapple with vagueness. The actual encounter with the light box is not emphasized in this second cycle, as it copies the first cycle of data and seems to be approaching data saturation. The students had the same difficulty describing what they saw, and agreed that different perspectives changed the result inside the lightbox.

> NaSa: when the mirror gets smaller, the light reflect more and the color gets mixed. Makes it have more color

> NaSa notices that things change as the mirrors get smaller, just like in the first cycle.
> Strangely, there was more disbelief in the experiment than the first cycle, as in this example:

> Boy: "Because he (indicates the author) makes us see more color

Another difference was it was realized that the community of inquiry is too hard to develop with just one session. It was decided to keep the students in their teacher-centered desk organization after the encounter with the light box, not in a circle. The discussion did seem less lively in general, perhaps as a result. The kids were often quiet and waiting for the teacher to tell them what was going on, as described in the numerous occasions where the teacher speaking resulted in a response of silence and waiting from the kids.
The focus for the second cycle is in the discussion:

It seems that in the discussion we got down to the essential question that the light box exercise was trying to ask. In this, I believe the 2nd cycle discussion was a success.

Teacher: and then when you look at two by two you see more color and then when you look at the 1x1 you see lots of color. Remember the picture I showed you, there was white in the middle right? Why is there white in the middle, because we didn't shine white light.
Teacher: is that white real?
Kids sit upright: (inaudible)
Boy: "its real"

During the discussion of the 2nd cycle, the desire for doing more experimentation was palpable. We had to bring the mirrors out over and over again so the kids could look for clues as to why the size of the mirrors made colors mix more. They really wanted to use a magnifying glass, at first they did not believe that magnifying the 1x1 mirror 300% would make you see the same as looking at the 4x4 mirror. Finally, after trying to use the teacher glasses as a magnifying glass, they decided to try to use their imagination, instead of looking at the mirrors in front of them. It was reiterated by the students that magnifying the 1x1 mirror to look bigger would yield more color than looking at the actually bigger mirror surfaces (which yields less colors). This indicates that in their struggle to explain the vagueness, they agreed that vagueness can be looked at more closely, it does not disappear to a further-away or smaller level as you look more closely.

However, this opinion became rather confused over the course of the discussion. The first (apparent) change in opinion is marked in this example:

Teeko: its (talking about magnification) not real, its fake ["Lokta"-blurry, not real, fake, illusion] (hes talking about the big mirror, [confusing with magnification?]) "it doesn't make you see more color"
Teacher: ok like when you look at the bigger mirror, do you see more color?
Bin: no, the smaller one has more color.
Teacher: yeah the smaller one has more color right?
Kids agree
Teacher: yeah so when we use the magnifying glass to look at the smaller one..
Bin: You see the color is the same, you don't see more color

141

Teacher: hmm the same color?

It is difficult to know of they mean the same color as the mirror-size they are looking at (magnified) or the same color as the larger mirror (not actually magnified but looking the same as the magnified one). I think they mean that magnification would not yield fewer colors, as looking at an (actually) larger mirror would yield. They then elaborated that magnification:

> Bin still wants to say something
> Bin: They're the same color, but when we magnify we see more
> clearly but we might see color we can't see (without magnification)

So rather than seeing less color, as the experiment seems to suggest, magnification yields the "same" color, that is, it would not change the image of more colors visible without the magnifying glass, and it may even make more colors visible. This is the opposite conclusion to what the experiment actually suggests. They believe (quite independently of the experiment) that magnification makes colors more visible, not less. However the experiment shows that color can only be visible when vagueness allows the colors to be mixed. Magnification separates colors. When colors are separated and there are only three original colored lights, this separation results in fewer visible colors. However a different experiment could be imagined where they are right—where looking closer would yield more colors visible. That is less interesting than the students insistence in denying their senses in the case of this experiment, in favor of a tacit belief that magnification yields more "information" or colors, not less.

For the student who used the very interesting Thai word "Lokta" it is unclear if he means the actually larger mirrors or the magnification of smaller mirrors to look like larger mirrors, he seems to be confusing them together, and claiming that the result of seeing at this level is an illusion. Now, does this mean that magnifying does not reveal? That it actually produces an illusion? The word Lokta seems to be getting used in the opposite way to what it normally means. Things are blurry when they are distant or small, or not magnified. As a result, his contribution is so confused it does not lend itself to analysis. It is a perfect example of the persistence of vagueness.

> Bin: I think their both real, its just that we stay in the far distance, so we see less, when we use microscope we see more.

5.3 Summary of Findings

Vagueness is initially very surprising, but with time the surprise is covered up by a theory. In this case, Gus and Bright appear comfortable with their theories. Gus seems to think that the "normal" color is not real, but "we can't tell what color it is", that the multicolored (vague) view is "real" and "normal" is an illusion. This is the usual rhetorical effect of a scientific "experiment". Even though in the moment of experiencing the "real" Gus couldn't tell (or write) what he experienced. In spite of this experience Gus continues to believe that there is an objective reality out of reach from what we can perceive with "normal" means.

Do students progress from physical/mechanical considerations to philosophical discussion on the concepts contained in these physical/mechanical stimulus (e.g. vagueness and logical pluralism) and if so, how? Is it different from reading stimulus? Students didn't seem to wax philosophical, or they did so without realizing the significance of what they were saying. In the second intervention students did acquire a certain philosophical "intensity" when asked if the things they saw were "real" or illusions.

In opposition to Sprod's finding:

> An unanticipated result of the study was the suggestion that triggers based on stories may be more effective in encouraging student reasoning about science than those based on 'surprising' experiments." (Sprod as quoted in Moriyon 2012, p94)

The excitement of students deemed "bad," especially when they realized there was no 'right answer' suggests that this kind of activity would be good for students with a variety of backgrounds and abilities. Looking from different angles changes what you see in the light box is the very thing than would make most scientific experiments unscientific (but not one investigating vagueness specifically). This investigation gave students the opportunity to evaluate a complex situation for themselves, without the teacher waiting expectantly for the right answer.

The finding that reached saturation is the students complaints that they can't write it down, and their desire to look long and look again at the more vague rough mirrors in the light box. Students want to use their senses more with the absence of a clear application of a theory. The central finding presented here is that vagueness is the part of inquiry that (at least initially) defies theory application. As such vagueness is unfiltered experience.

Conclusion

> Science uses terms more precisely than ordinary language, and I am not sure that science teaching at present allows students to grasp these differences properly. This leads to confusion. Take the word 'work.' I could sit here with my eyes closed, thinking hard about how to answer your questions: in everyday language, we would say I was doing a lot of work. In physics, though, there would be virtually no work done. Science is full of such key concepts: energy, species, light, bonds, elasticity. Many are ordinary words, but with special conceptual meanings. (Sprod 2017)

Work is an important idea in pragmatism, and can be seen as an ultimate concept in physics:

> Concerning the basic law of motion, the law of inertia, the question arises whether this law is not to be subordinated under a more general one, i.e., the law of conservation of energy, which is now determined according to its expenditure and consumption, as work, . . . questionability is concealed by the results and the progress of scientific work." (Heidegger 1977, p. 270)

But conservation of energy can be called into question, for example, energy can "degrade," making it less able to do work. When energy has degraded a lot, so that it cannot do work anymore, can it said to be "conserved?"

Peirce claims that uncertainty is an uncomfortable, unsatisfying disposition, and because of this, we are directed to work. We must work until we know, but vagueness is always there at the edges of our knowledge. Must we always be dissatisfied then?

The light box is an experiment because it appears to reveal "the truth" as a contrived and removed from the "normal." The vague situation is what the lightbox contrives to show, it is the truth removed from the normal even though vague situations are common in everyday life. The message is that in scientific investigation we are in a world of vagueness, not precision, just like we are outside scientific investigation. Being dissatisfied with vagueness means being dissatisfied both with our scientific findings and everyday life.

When all you desire to satisfy your curiosity is precision or clarity, the ultimate question becomes "how": how do I make my measurements/terms more precise? Technique, in proof and measurement apparatus, becomes tantamount. However, vagueness is persistent no matter how precise you get. Raising vagueness, recognizing and acknowledging vagueness fundamentally changes the prevailing kind of scholarship that is required.

If you make an idea clearer, do you change it? At first he could not have given the same explanation of his method...he had a rough idea...so we may say his idea changed....The question is: Why should we call this new idea a clarification of the old one? We might say instead that later on he tried to solve a different problem...—You might say he has been led to change his question" (Wittgenstein 1976, p88)

6.1 Vagueness: an interdisciplinary theory

An interdisciplinary approach to education is an imperative. Take Latour's example of how a synthesis of disciplines (from different sciences to politics) is needed just to read the daily newspaper.

"This would be a hopeless dilemma had anthropology not accustomed us t o deali ng ca lml y a nd straightforwardly with the seamless fabric of what I shall call 'nature-culture'...Once she has been sent into the field, even the most rationalist ethnographer is perfectly capable of bringing together in a single monograph the myths, ethnosciences, religions, epics and rites of the people she is studying... is only because they separate at home that ethnographers make so bold as to unify abroad." (Latour 2002, p7)

Students need connections between disciplines first. The more precise and technical definitions can come after such a synthesis where the borderlines between disciplines are vague. The need for a philosophical element in science teaching has also attracted increasing support, Shayer and Adey (1981, p. 150) call on teachers to "take a view of science which is more that of a philosopher than of the professional scientist." Further, the need to infuse science teaching with material from the history and philosophy of science, in order to deepen children's understanding of the nature of science, has been argued by many (e.g., Matthews, 1992; Sprod 1993)."(Sprod 1998, p465)

Vagueness is usually recognized as a philosophical problem. The disciplines touched on in this multi-disciplinary study are physical science, math and philosophy. The physicality of the light box is troubling: if vagueness must be classified as purely philosophical, then it seems that some physical considerations are not scientific at all.

The reason vagueness is so troubling is its relationship with (and definition by) logic. In the next quote Dewey asserts that logic is philosophy, of course, it is also math, so we have the first connection between math and philosophy for free. logic is a branch of philosophic theory; so that different views of its subject-matter are expressions of different ultimate philosophies,"(Dewey 1938, Loc. 131-132) Next, Dewey connects philosophy with science.

> "...Dewey used primary experience and secondary experience as a means to compare philosophic method with scientific method. He argued that philosophy needs to follow the empirical method, as science does, because he thought that science not only draws its material from primary experience, but also refers primary experience back again to test a scientific theory (LW 1)."(Na, Song 2014, p 1034)

Philosophy is perfected through a process of noting experience and reflecting on it, comparing the result of reflection with experience—like science. Vagueness fits in where Dewey talks about primary experience, which is always vague. It is almost as if the "refinement" Dewey is talking about is the removal of vagueness from primary experience. If vagueness is the focus of the study, however, the whole process is at odds with itself. This is the purpose of choosing vagueness as a focus of a scientific/philosophical experiment, to trouble Dewey's example of "normal" philosophy or science. It doesn't matter if we call vagueness scientific or philosophical experience, its just experience. The reason it is so difficult to categorize is vagueness is exactly what needs to be removed to fit things into categories. Vagueness is exactly the thing that sits between our nice categorizations, causing trouble.

I found that in my own experiment with P4 students, that they would sometimes say things that were problematic, and the problems would either be philosophical or physical ("Its the color of a mirror") or both ("When I change my perspective, the colors change") but there would be no tension in the students discussions. The problems they presented were unwitting and left uncontested by other students.

> In many science lessons, philosophical questions lie relatively close to the surface, but they are not often addressed. Such questions include the nature of truth and proof, the relationship between theories and observations, the role of idealisation in science, the nature and use of classification schemes and so on."
> (Sprod 1998, p464)

The teacher noted that when certain students learned there was no "right answer" to the light box activity, they became really excited. The transcript attests to the surprise and excitement of the students, and there were several instances, even though this was not a focus of the study, of students asserting that the answer depended on your perspective: 2 in transcript1, 6 in transcript 2, but in response one teacher questions in both cycles on whether different students can see different things, many students nod in assent to this. Investigating vagueness (between the reflection theory and the light-scattering theory) there really is no right answer. That is why it is a real example of a question. Vagueness is a physical phenomenon and belongs to scientific, mathematical and philosophical considerations. It is the exception to Sprod's finding that:

> "...different styles of facilitation may be necessary for discussions based on stories and those based on surprising experiments; the former being better for the development of scientific thinking." (Sprod 1998, p476)

6.2 Creating a subjectivity

"Space is your mind" -Alan Watts

Space is your mind in that your mind contains or reflects everything that enters it, except education builds a filter for this mind/space, allowing only certain things in and making other things invisible. So when we talk about Euclidean geometry, which is about space, we are really talking about a filter that only allows things in that are measurable with a ruler, things that have measure according to number. Learning that Euclidean geometry is the one true geometry (done for thousands of years in the west and still done in my own experience by other teachers working with me) makes things that are not measurable invisible to us.

Education creates a certain subjectivity (an unnecessary one because there is also non-euclidean geometry, and other filters even, besides geometry)

Vagueness is when someone questions their current filter, looking outside, or just on the edge, of what their word-filter allows to be visible, and tries to make the invisible visible for a moment. The attitude towards vagueness, generalizations, and logic are important epistemic choices for any cultural subjectivity.

"Practically all our words are generic to a greater or lesser extent, yet there is a great deal of variation between different languages: some seem to favour particular terms while others lean towards the abstract and general type. For a long time it was customary for linguists, psychologists and anthropologists to regard the languages of primitive races as rich in specific terms and poor in generic ones. This was commonly interpreted as
• sign of 'pre-logical mentality', ..The Zulus, for instance, were reported to have no word for 'cow', only specific expressions for 'red cow', 'white cow', etc. Unfortunately, however, the evidence is suspect;" (Ullmann 1972, p120)

"...in all the languages we know, a word for "all" but not for "all but one". This is enormously important: this sort of fact which characterizes our logic. "All but one" seems to us a complex idea —"all", that's a simple idea. But we can imagine a tribe where "all but one" is the primitive idea. And this sort of thing would entirely change their outlook on logic." (Wittgenstein 1976, p193)

One problem with math is, pragmatically speaking, it turns people into tools, which may be pragmatically useful, but is still unethical. We don't want to use people pragmatically, but "use" is the ultimate concept in pragmatism. And education seems to follow suit, after all, the current state of education is heavily dominated by corporate influence that tries to render students not just useful for jobs in their corporate body, but unable to imagine a different power structure. Other power structures are filtered out.

We can see the results of this corporate influence in Trickey an Topping (2004): "Given these encouraging findings, why is P4C not more firmly embedded in teacher development and routine classroom practice?" p377 Biesta (2011) critiques humanism by saying that humanism "isn't human enough", because it tries to proclaim universally what a human is, when all humans have a uniqueness that is part of what makes them human. The human subject is sometimes considered an educational goal. When we promote thinking skills are we aimed at "'production' of a particular kind of subjectivity."?

> "From an educational point of view the problem with humanism is that is specifies a norm of what it means to be human before the actual manifestation of 'instances' of humanity. It specifies what the child, student or newcomer must become before giving them an opportunity to show who they are and who they will be (see also Vansieleghem, 2005)." (Biesta 2011, loc 4419)

That paraconsistent logic can be programmed into a computer (see previous posted video of said program) means that technology can be "illogical" in a classical sense, and cannot be taken to signify the success of logic. Now what kind of subjectivity would a self-contradictory logic create? On the benefit of logical pluralism- is it just another kind of "machinery" that kids adopt instead of thinking for themselves? How does logical pluralism undermine machinery? Logical pluralism and vagueness are theories that give students a choice about what to filter and what not. We choose one logic and certain things are visible, switch to another and other things are visible. Using one logic over another will have an effect on our behavior, but ultimately the machinery of a particular logic is not the point. *Choosing* between logics is the point.

The ultimate concept is not the pragmatic "use" but merely the question "Which?" and in answering which, we take into account the situation, and the other questions of importance to us from "Who, what, when, where, why" and of course "how" is still available to us, though no longer the ultimate question. Ultimately the power of choosing or creating your own logic, is an existential choice—such a power can and should be given to our students. We should not be dictating to them what it is to be human, or subjecting them to corporate need.

6.3 Questioning the ultimate concept of Difference Logical pluralism as the field of mathematics where Difference (as the Peircian graphs show is the fundamental concept of classical logic) is split into differences (The other logics). differences with a small "d" shouldn't be spoken of in generalizations. Difference the general concept should never be spoken, and yet here are places I have found it written: "The development of the general ability for independent thinking and judgement should always be placed foremost. Not the acquisition of special knowledge." (Einstein 1950)

The word is missing, but the basic idea is, if "I think therefore I am" then he wants people to "be different." This is the subjectivity that Einstein wants education to produce. The specific context of how they are different is less important than just being different.

"Therein lies the main significance of promoting philosophical experiences with teachers and students—not to legitimate what we or they know, but to foster difference in their thinking and our thinking as well." (Kohan 2011, Kindle Loc 5219)

Here the all-important "s"—differences—is missing. Kohan (2012) tries to get at this metaphysical essence of difference, calling it the essence of philosophy, but Karaba (2012) criticizes him,

> In other words, with this statement he insinuates that real philosophy, and the real teaching of philosophy, is, and should be, devoid of ethical and political aims. Thus, this view assumes a kind of neutrality in philosophy and philosophical education. If this is what Kohan means by teaching philosophy in "empty spaces" then he positions philosophy itself as having a metaphysical essence to be discovered.2" (Karaba 2012, p53)

The metaphysical essence is "Difference". Karaba evokes Dewey to help the above (and more) better understand Difference as differences.

> Deweyan pragmatism does not shy away from, but embraces the ethical, political, and aesthetic dimensions. Aims in any kind of education are not amoral and apolitical, just as philosophy itself is not amoral and apolitical. Dewey's philosophy shifts the focus of inquiry from discovery of True philosophy and the True aim of philosophical education to the ethical, political, and aesthetic uses of aims in education for particular purposes by particular people." (Karaba 2012, p53)

differences becomes "special" to circumstances, so with that already done by Dewey, do we need the ultimate concept of Difference to be divided "ultimately" in addition to asserting that differences are special? Do we need logical pluralism?

I think we do. Difference appears to be a concept in itself. In Plato's Sophist "not-being" was one of five ultimate concepts in a philosophical system, which took the place of difference as a separation between beings. (Hence Kohan's reference to "empty spaces" and my inference that he is talking about Difference.) It is a confusion that language seems to confound. (Did the previous authors intend to sound as though they were talking about Difference instead of differences, or is it just semantics?) And since, as is explored a lot here, vagueness is an empirically based counter-example against an ultimate concept "Difference" that motivates logical pluralism, Difference as an ultimate concept should be brought down, and the concepts that will do it are "differences" and vagueness.

> The interest of the individual in the improved management of his own life must be acknowledged to have first priority, for we can have no better incentive than to see our lives improve upon our thinking them through." Lipman 1988 loc 102

The individual identity is the place where synthesis is allowed. We are allowed to identify with ideas, things, people and places, experiences, sexuality, and bundle them together into a notion of self. It may be argued that vagueness is not a transcendental concept, that it is not "out there" but only an error made by individuals. However the same error is made in order to synthesize an individual. In other words, the "error" is prior to the individual. One must first err in thinking of having a self, a vague synthesis of likes a dislikes, beliefs and prejudices. It cannot be the self that errs, and vagueness is not a result of subjectivity, even though our judgement of vagueness can easily be the result of, as Raffman (1994) puts it, "psychological states". That vagueness is error is not supported here, I am merely using the language of moderns, as Foucault puts it, likeness is the occasion of error, not a source of knowledge for moderns. It is not an error to bundle together a self, depending on the self so bundled. This paragraph is merely a description of what is normally allowed under the current regime of precision knowledge.

While identity politics is outside the scope of this study, something must be said on how vagueness relates to formulating a self. If we continually look more closely at ourselves to define ourselves, we will find the concepts we use to describe ourselves are vague, and the modern tendency is to be unsatisfied with that.

A valueless, objective source for knowledge is one that asserts itself as the only one of its kind. This is why logical pluralism (as opposed to classical or modern logical monism) is a revolutionary topic. "…Channell (1994) puts it vagueness 'often plays an important part in the act of meaning'." (Rowland 2000) Domination can become apparent in the expectation that propositions have only one clear and distinct meaning (that vagueness does not enter), doing away with the creativity in meaning construction, with the allowance of difference in worldview from varying interpretations. Meaning isn't and shouldn't be communicated perfectly, what matters is that there is some communication, that the two (more) meanings of a single proposition overlap to some degree, shared by many differing peoples. Relevant logic can be singled out as explicitly handling a kind of relativism, where logical laws only hold if they are specific to a "situation" which could easily be applied to a "culture." Brouwer still upholds constructive logic to be about "universal" intuition. The pluralism taught does not end definitively, but instead allows for more logics yet uninvented. Freedom is a self-contradictory concept—one must have control of oneself in order to be free to do what one wants—but the author has endeavored here to show how freedom is fostered by attention to vagueness and logical pluralism.

6.4 An idea for a new logic

For Dewey, "Since the time of Aristotle, the nugatory nature of "infinitation of the negative" has been generally recognized." (Kindle Locations 3292-3300 Dewey 1938). This kind of theory of negation forces empirical study, because empty formal calculation cannot be done without a definition of negation that is less divergent. One way to control the "infinitation of the negative" is to introduce a symbol that is the opposite of modern negation.

For example, take the logical statements
(A) ~[q->(p AND r)]
(B) [q AND ~(p AND r)]
and
(C) q AND ~p OR ~r
Even though in modern logic these statements are said to be equivalent, they are actually different.
In English, (A) is the set of all things that are NOT the statement "If I have to go then I am going home and I am eating cake", which includes you, me, my community, ?
However the set of all things that are (B) "I have to go and NOT the statement "I am going home and I am eating cake" includes less than the previous statement[2], but still more than the next statement:
(C) "I have to go and I am not going home or I am not eating cake."
The question is expansive and inclusive; it is the opposite of the modern "not" operation. The following example is merely a mathematized play to show the power of inquiry. Maybe a "?" would push out the "not" one level in the statement. The ? Symbol means to factor out the negation symbol one step. For example If we have "(q AND ~p OR ~r)?" that is the same as (B): [q AND ~(p AND r)] and the statement suffers from some "infinitation of the negative," but less than (A) does.

6.5 Vagueness as the incarnation of inquiry

When the students encountered vagueness, their response was to investigate very intensely with their eyes. It took prompting for them to rely on their imagination of further experiments using magnification, and other, unplanned sensory investigation took place at the desire of the students. This suggests that vagueness is importantly tied to the bodily senses. Vagueness is an embodiment because, when moving, say, from the top of a mountain that we category "high up" to a valley we category as "not high up", we could not traverse the vague height where we are unsure whether we are high up or not without leaving our abstractions and experiencing this traversal with our bodies/senses.

When we started we knew where we were, as we walked down gradually we had to accept that we didn't know which category we fit into, and had to use our senses as the basis of knowledge, instead of categories and analysis. No matter how much we know or theorize, or investigate with the senses, our incarnated minds are involved in an unknown, an embodied inquiry. This is not Shapiro's (2006) thesis that context is the answer the problem, mainly because Shapiro's "context" is one in a conversational language game, and, as he says, is only a model. The offering made here is that there is no model for vagueness, it is, "truly" unsettled and unsolvable. Vagueness is the opposite of categorization, that is how it is analyzed in Keefe's (2000) book, yet it is also immediately physical. The presence and awareness of our bodies ensouls the analytical, logical, categorical tendencies of the mind, and with this ensoulment comes vagueness, the irrational, the imperfect and incomplete. While vagueness is not a subjective problem, as stated before, neither are our bodies subjective. Awareness of the body is just in the middle between subjectivity and objectivity—a place where vagueness between these categories can be explored.

Vagueness is therefore part of human experience, it is not a celestial fantasy as Russell admits the purely logical is, it is the result of looking for this fantasy in the matter at hand. The earthly experience of our bodies brings encounters with conflict. We are hungry but overweight, we are tired but excited, we want to be in a particular place, a particular yoga pose, but our bodies are too big or small, too inflexible, to fit exactly into what the mind envisions. This embodiment is how we traverse a mountain, starting from high up and moving outside what are minds can categorize, it is how Zeno's paradoxes of motion are avoided, and motion continues—because we do not really understand motion with points on a trajectory, we understand motion with our bodies. The "point" or perfectly defined "position" on a real number line is utterly supernatural and unrealistic.

Attention to vagueness takes us out of scholastic exercises and puts us back in our bodies. Students are compelled to look and look again at the light box, they are compelled to break the formulas of classical logic and pay attention to the context they are in right now. Not because context "solves" vagueness, but context is where we experience and experience vagueness. Does context really remove the contradictions of the senses? With the example of the light box, the mirrors make different contexts available: they are like magnifications of each other, and the same trouble of vagueness is there with the knowledge of other magnifications/contexts.

Vagueness becomes immediately present with embodiment, it becomes apparent when our embodiment is investigated. Some (Peirce, Shapiro) believe that vagueness is a kind of indeterminacy that is not satisfactory. Their minds need clarity and distinctness to feel they understand. Without this desire for clarity, vagueness would not be apparent, we would just have experience. Vagueness is when, looking for distinctness and clarity, we find the indistinct and the blurry. Without this inquiry that is guided by the needs of the mind, and directed to the bodily senses, vagueness does not become apparent. When the mind explores vagueness in a general way, abstracted from other senses, the mind is being used like a bodily sense. After all, even though it can have passions for clear understanding, the mind is embodied too and it ought to be capable of imagining vagueness without the aid of other senses (the mind may envision vagueness with the visual part of the brain without using the eyes, for example).

Vagueness is the result of empirical inquiry with analytical or rational expectations. It is tied up in the difference and similarities between math and science, between a calculation and an experiment. Investigating using categories is a kind of recognition of what is given to the senses. Without this recognition, it is recognized to be vague. Now, when we do an experiment, we set up a contrivance and the result is not known, not immediately recognizable. The experiment is usually contrived to avoid vagueness, but must still encounter (initially) unrecognizable results if the experiment is interesting.

As in Wittgenstein, a mathematical calculation is not
an experiment

> "If we said, "Let's see what happens when we multiply
> 136 by 51", it may be an experiment—but it isn't clear
> what experiment. I may want to see if you can multiply
> correctly, or to see if the chalk will stand the
> strain...Now an experiment has a result. So does a
> calculation. If one calls something the result of the
> calculation, is that same thing the result of the
> experiment? Watson: Not necessarily.
> Wittgenstein: No, not necessarily—but is it even
> possibly? Turing has called the calculation an
> experiment... I might say I made an experiment to see
> what he would write down in the end. The result of the
> experiment is then: that he wrote down 6936. But if this
> is an experiment, could you say that the experiment
> was wrong if he wrote down 6935? If I am merely
> trying to find out by experiment what he will write
> down, it does not matter what he writes down."
> (Wittgenstein 1976, p93-94)

I believe that is why the encounter with the light box is
interesting to the students. It involves math but is not a
calculation and is still an experiment, it involves science but
without a technical "right answer." It involves students in
theorizing without leading them into one theory or another. This
is why even scientific investigation, not just bodily
investigation, is an encounter with vagueness—with the
indeterminacy of the senses (an indeterminacy that is only
present when the mind is looking for determinacy).

It was hypothesized that vagueness, especially explored in
a community, gives rise to questioning. This seems to be slightly
off, it does not give rise to questioning, it does give rise inquiry in
the form of theorizing and much more investigation. Vagueness,
a natural tendency for the senses to disagree with the analytical
mind, draws the inquirer into more inquiry. Dewey realized that
inquiry is the source of logical laws.

> Logic is autonomous. The position taken implies the ultimacy of inquiry in determination of the formal conditions of inquiry. Logic as inquiry into inquiry is, if you please, a circular process; it does not depend upon anything extraneous to inquiry. The force of this proposition may perhaps be most readily understood by noting what it precludes. It precludes the determination and selection of logical first principles by an a priori intuitional act," (Dewey 1938, Locations 431-435)

Before the law of contradiction, there is inquiry. And before the law of contradiction, all is vague, according to Peirce's definition of vagueness. Vagueness and inquiry are prior to any formalized logic, but that does not mean that vagueness and inquiry are prior to form. Vagueness would not be available without the expectation within the mind of whatever forms or categories it chooses to grasp with towards the deliverances of the senses. This is how vagueness depends on both empirical and rational tendencies. Dewey holds that logic must have empirical grounds, and the ground is always vague.

The position here taken holds that they [logical forms] are intrinsically postulates of and for inquiry, being formulations of conditions, discovered in the course of inquiry itself, which further inquiries must satisfy if they are to yield warranted assert ability as a consequence." (Dewey 1938, Loc 357-359)

Turning to logical pluralism, as a result of vagueness being an integral part of inquiry, one logic is not enough. Conflicting information is not merely an academic, abstract monster, but arises in our experience constantly, logical pluralism arises from inquiry naturally. Any one logic is purely hypothetical, and does not exclude the possibility of other logics. any statement that logic is so-and-so, can, in the existing state of logical theory, be offered only as a hypothesis and an indication of a position to be developed." (Dewey 1938 Loc141-142)

The law of contradiction is only a hypothesis, it is not a law, and it is clear that the hypothesis is refuted in many situations, such as any time language is used (all language is vague). The hypothesis is challenged and not fully applicable.

How do these theoretical considerations come to bear on education? The claim is that awareness of vagueness finds its first home in the body, in the way the body fails to respond perfectly to the expectations of the analytical mind. The body and the expectations extend to the physical world, and the analytical world of mathematics. To teach how mathematics fails to be at home in the body, and how vagueness succeeds in this manner, is to entrust students to begin their own cycle of inquiry, grounded in the senses, and fueled by the dissatisfaction of the mind.

> [P4C aims to]...elicit the contestable within the commonly accepted unproblematic. For example, the concept of "wetness" is introduced in the elementary curriculum and it is explored by considering examples of things that are wet and not wet. The problematic is introduced when children are asked to decide whether things like moist, foggy, damp, and humid are things that are wet, not wet, neither or both. And similarly, whether it is raining or not might, at first, seem unproblematic. But in this curriculum children are directed to the problematic with questions like, "What if there are just one or two drops, is it raining?" (Gazzard 1993, p628)

Gazzard's examples are physical. They are not technical or abstract, and are available to the young. Inquiry at this level is just as perplexing and conducive to important knowledge and wisdom as more technical, abstract, or analytical considerations. Vagueness is at the limits of our knowledge, and is also what we have to begin with, this realization both invites a state of rest, and puts the responsibility for inquiry on the shoulders of the child, not on big science apparatus.

6.6 The call to rest

To understand vagueness as physical incarnation of inquiry, and to understand that inquiry is prior even to logical "laws" or hypotheses, undermines the idea of progress that is prevalent in pragmatism. At the limits of your inquiry you find vagueness, which is what we had at the beginning. While perhaps there is a qualified kind of progress in inquiry, (and such progress is importantly not "the only" way to progress, since there are many logics/paths and another logic/another path could crop up anytime), ultimately we find what we began with: inquiry. Dewey affirms that inquiry into inquiry is circular, depending only on empirical matters of concern. He still believes that progress is achieved. I agree that qualified, non-unique, progress is achieved, but it is not the point. The point is happiness, and if you are happy before you go searching through inquiry for some kind of progress or resolution, there is no need to pursue such inquiry.

> Logic is a progressive discipline. The reason for this is that logic rests upon analysis of the best methods of inquiry (being judged "best" by their results with respect to continued inquiry) As the methods of the sciences improve, corresponding changes take place in logic." (Dewey 1938, loc 323-325)

The basic observation here is that vagueness is "deeper" than knowledge. No matter how completely inquiry describes a situation "as a whole" just a little deeper there is vagueness. Of course this is not saying much, just like the word "knowledge" does not say much. Both concepts are empty and need filling as to what is vague/known and how so. It should be mentioned in the same breath that a limit to vagueness must be acknowledged, however, this limit is purely ethical. It is ethical because when happiness is achieved further inquiry is unethical.

> "Students with a bag full of skills are not going to perform well in science or function well later on as professional scientists if they are not motivated or inspired to inquire in the first place. Science education then, needs also to stimulate inquiry." (Gazzard 1993, p627)

What can we take from this quote: are students not inquisitive enough? or are they just not inquisitive in the way we want, e.g. in the way that scientists have gone? In ways we think are fruitful? It is not enough to uphold just inquiry. Inquiry has a form in the cultures and disciplines in which it is employed, even though it is corrosive to such forms. Inquiry should be guided and limited, not just stimulated without end. I have offered that vagueness is a source of problems for a concept, it is at the boundaries of a concept, its fuzzy connections to other concepts, as well it is at the boundary between the word and the external objective reality referred. In a science classroom, things like conservation of energy is taught, but not problematized.

As even Sprod (1994), one of the few published in advocating for P4C (Philosophy for Children) in science learning, argued that physical experiments cannot be problematized the same way a concept can. Reading a casual encounter with the tentative nature of inductive reasoning, necessary to infer that a scientific experiment can generally be duplicated, makes it easier for students to wax philosophical in whole class discussions. However the purpose is not to generate unease with what is known, but to trouble the current system of knowledge that drives us to work and push the boundaries of our amassed knowledge. The call is not for more work in the area of vagueness, except that work that draws into question the ultimate value of work itself. Logic 'ought' not be employed without end, just as a never-ending sequence such as the decimal expansion of pi ought not to be made ever more precise. But pluralism can suggest that there are other normative to logic.

> "The view rests on an idea that is sometimes captured with the slogan that logic is normative, where this means, roughly, that logic has consequences for how we ought to reason. Now suppose that the correct view about epistemic normativity is itself a pluralist one, and in particular, that the 'ought' in 'how we ought to reason', like many modal operators, can be disambiguated in several correct ways. Then it seems that there might also be multiple correct logics, corresponding to the multiple epistemic 'oughts'." (Russell 2013)

Pluralism opens the possibility of stopping this imperative of classical logic that our terms must be ever more distinct, because we 'ought' to get some rest and explore the meanings and interpretations of the knowledge we already have. The diluting effect of logical pluralism on logic in general brings doubt into our never-ending calculation of pi. And that doubt can lead to an end of such work.

"All that I wish to do by this is show that there are all sorts of different ways in which we could do logic or mathematics." (Wittgenstein 1976, p190)

6.7 How innovations speak

"...some gentlemen proclaim the right to have an independent opinion, in a closed space, the laboratory, over which the State has no control. And when these troublemakers find themselves in agreement, it is not on the basis of a mathematical demonstration that everyone would be compelled to accept, but on the basis of experiments observed by the deceptive senses, ... we are going to have to put up with this new clique of scholars who are going to start challenging everyone's authority in the name of Nature by invoking wholly fabricated laboratory events! If you allow the vacuum to be infiltrated into the air pump and, from there, into natural philosophy, then you will divide authority again: the immaterial spirits will incite everyone to revolt by offering a court of appeal for frustrations. Knowledge and Power will be separated once more." (Latour 2002, p20)

Interestingly, Knowledge became Power when scientists were elevated to the high priesthood of society. Here we see a struggle between the old sources of power and the scientists for power. The scientists are pretending to only struggle for knowledge, but as Latour deftly reveals, this struggle is very much a political struggle for power.

How do the light box and logic puzzle fit in? The light box makes the focus concept of the experiment vagueness, which challenges a certain kind of knowledge, knowledge in the form of precision. Foucault mentions that the modern version of knowledge, in the form of precision and difference, was preempted by a knowledge of various similitudes. Vagueness could be seen as what remains of this previous kind of knowledge. A vagueness between two things is like a synthesis between these two things. You cannot tell how they are separate, therefore they are joined until further investigation.

It is importantly a physical synthesis, easily in the realm of physics. In that sense, it is subversive to the high priests of science, but it is not subversive to acquiring knowledge. Vagueness has the strength of not being divisive the way precision is. Logical pluralism may seem to respond to vagueness calling for greater precision, but actually what it does is dilute precision and the difference-form of knowledge by dividing the usual method of excavating clear and distinct concepts: logical deduction. Logical deduction is divided, diluting its power. Precision knowledge has a way of dividing people, and this is why it is uplifted by those in power, not because it is a superior kind of knowledge. The innovations found here will not be uplifted, even though, as Latour writes: "While moderns insure themselves by not thinking at all about the consequences of their innovations for the social order, the premoderns—if we are to believe the anthropologists—dwell endlessly and obsessively on those connections between nature and culture. To put it crudely: those who think the most about hybrids circumscribe them as much as possible, whereas those who choose to ignore them ...develop them to the utmost." (Latour 2002, p41)

In other words, premoderns think before adding innovations to their society, moderns don't. Scientific innovations are apolitical, they are transcendent and therefore do not enter into the realm of their much needed social approval or denial. But this is quite far from the truth, and therefore we are not modern. Vagueness is largely ignored as a source of knowledge, logical pluralism is an abstract entertainment of a few scholars, not a widespread educational enterprise, and P4C, despite its many successes reported in scholarly literature, is not nearly as widespread as it ought to be. (Trickey an Topping 2004) Instead, education is the means of producing subjectivities that filter out the innovations that demur.

> "we live in communities whose social bond comes from objects fabricated in laboratories; ideas have been replaced by practices, apodictic reasoning by a controlled doxa, and universal agreement by groups of colleagues." (Latour 2002, p21-22 my emphasis)

An innovation is a new technology inviting a new practice, and new practices are the new ideas.

> "With Boyle and his successors, we begin to conceive of what a natural force is, an object that is mute but endowed or entrusted with meaning." (Latour 2002, p29)

That is why the I offer the ideas of vagueness and logical pluralism in the form of an innovative scientific experiment and a web app. The rough mirrors are inert bodies endowed with a kind of ignorance, an unthinking that is mistaken for honesty. The subversion of "(precision) knowledge is power" is found in vagueness, which direct students to explore with their senses and disbelieve the filters that make vagueness invisible or ignored. A logical pluralism web app innovation, if it is endowed with meaning, is a way of speaking out against precision knowledge and its divisive power over people.

References

1 Abbott, S., (2001). Understanding Analysis. New York, NY. Springer Science+Business Media, Inc.

2 Apostle, H. (1980). Aristotle's Categories and Propositions (De interpretatione). Grinnell, Iowa: Peripatetic Press.

3 Aksu, G., & Koruklu, N. (2015). Determination the Effects of Vocational High School Students' Logical and Critical Thinking Skills on Mathematics Success. Eurasian Journal Of Educational Research (EJER), (59), 181-206. : 10.14689/ejer.2015.59.11

4 Allo, P., 2007, "Logical pluralism and semantic information," Journal of Philosophical Logic, 38(6): 659–694.

5 Barnes, J. (1984). The complete works of Aristotle: The revised Oxford translation. Princeton, N.J.: Princeton University Press.

6 Beall, J. (2013). A Simple Approach Towards Recapturing Consistent Theories In Paraconsistent Settings. The Review of Symbolic Logic, 6(04), 755-764. doi:10.1017/s1755020313000208

7 Beall, J., & Restall, G. (2006). Logical pluralism. Oxford: Clarendon Press ;.

8 Beall, J. & Restall, G. (2000) "Logical pluralism," Australasian Journal of Philosophy, 78: 475-493.

9 Beall, J. & Restall, G. (2001) "Defending logical pluralism," in Logical Consequence: Rival Approaches Proceedings of the 1999 Conference of the Society of Exact Philosophy, Stanmore: Hermes, pp. 1–22.

10 Biesta, G. (2011). Philosophy, Exposure, and Children: How to Resist the Instrumentalisation of Philosophy in Education. Journal of Philosophy of Education, 45(2), 305-319. doi:10.1111/j.1467-9752.2011.00792.x

11 Bishop, E. (1967). Foundations of constructive analysis. New York: McGraw-Hill.

12 Bouhnik, D., & Giat, Y. (2009). Teaching High School

166

Students Applied Logical Reasoning. Journal Of
Information Technology Education, 8IIP-1-IIP-16.

13 Bregant, J. (2014). Critical Thinking in Education: Why to
Avoid Logical Fallacies?. Problems Of Education In The
21St Century, 6118-27.

14 Brouwer, L. E., & Dalen, D. V. (1981). Brouwer's
Cambridge lectures on intuitionism. Cambridge:
Cambridge University Press.

15 Channell, J.M. (1994). Vague Language, Oxford,
Oxford University Press.

16 Carrier, J. (2014). Student Strategies Suggesting
Emergence of Mental Structures Supporting Logical
and Abstract Thinking: Multiplicative Reasoning.
School Science & Mathematics, 114(2), 87- 96.
doi:10.1111/ssm.12053

17 Damarin, S. (1999). Social Construction and Mathematics
Education: The Relevance of Theory. In L. Burton (Ed.),
Learning mathematics from hierarchies to networks.
London: Falmer.

18 DeLong, H. (1970). A profile of mathematical logic.
Reading, Mass.: Addison-Wesley   Pub.

19 Dewey, J. (1938). Logic, the theory of inquiry. New
York: H. Holt and Company.

20 Easwaran, E. (1987). The Dhammapada. London: Arkana.

22 Einstein (1950) Out of my later years. New York:
The Philosophical Library

23 Ernest, P. (1998). Social Constructivism as a Philosophy of
Mathematics. Albany,NY: State U of New York.

24 Ernest, P. (2008). Towards a Semiotics of Mathematical
Text (Part 1). For the Learning of Mathematics, 28(1),
2-8.Retrieved from http://www.jstor.org/stable/40248591

25 Ernest, P. (2009). Critical issues in mathematics
education. Charlotte, N.C.: IAP.

26 Edwards, P. (1972). The Encyclopedia of philosophy (Vol.
4-5). New York: Macmillan.

27 Ferreira, L. B. (2012). Philosophy for Children in Science
Class. Thinking: The Journal of Philosophy for Children,
20(1),   73-81. doi:10.5840/thinking2012201/211

28   Feyerabend, P., & Terpstra, B. (1999). Conquest of
      abundance: A tale of abstraction versus the richness of
      being. Chicago: University of Chicago Press.

29   Flegas, K., & Charalampos, L. (2013). Exploring Logical
      Reasoning and Mathematical Proof in Grade 6 Elementary
      School Students. Canadian Journal Of Science,
      Mathematics

29   Technology Education, 13(1), 70-89.
      doi:10.1080/14926156.2013.758326

30   Foucault, M. (1973). The order of things: An archaeology
      of the human sciences. New York: Vintage Books.

31   Gazzard, A. (1993). Thinking children and education
      (M. Lipman, Ed.). Dubuque, IA: Kendall/Hunt Pub. Co.

32   Gregory, A. (2017). Eureka!: The birth of science. London:
      Icon.

33   Glaser, B. G., & Strauss, A. L. (1967). The discovery of
      grounded theory: Strategies for   qualitative research.

34   Goddu, G. C. (2002) "What exactly is logical pluralism?"
      Australasian Journal of Philosophy, 80(2): 218–230.

35   Graff, D. (2001). Phenomenal Continua and the Sorites.
      Mind, 110(440), 905-936. doi:10.1093/mind/110.440.905

36   Hald, A. (2003). A history of probability and statistics and
      their applications before 1750. Hoboken, N.J.: Wiley.

37   Haynes, J., & Murris, K. (2011). Picturebooks,
      pedagogy and philosophy. New York: Routledge.

38   Hatzikiriakou, K., & Metallidou, P. (2009). Teaching
      Deductive Reasoning to Pre- service Teachers:
      Promises and Constraints. International Journal Of
      Science & Mathematics Education, 7(1), 81-101.
      doi:10.1007/s10763-007-9113-8

39   Karaba, R. (2012). Reconceptualizing the Aims in
      Philosophy for Children. Thinking: The Journal of
      Philosophy for Children, 20(1), 50-54.
      doi:10.5840/thinking2012201/27

40   Keefe, R. (2006). Theories of vagueness.
      Cambridge: Cambridge University Press.

41   Kohan, W. O. (2011). Childhood, Education and
      Philosophy: Notes on Deterritorialisation. Journal of
      Philosophy

of Education, 45(2), 339-357.doi:10.1111/j.1467-9752.2011.00796.x

42   Kuhn, T. S. (1970). The structure of scientific revolutions.Chicago: University of Chicago Press.

43   Lakatos, I. (1976). Proofs and refutations: The logic of mathematical discovery. Cambridge: Cambridge University Press.

44   Latour, B. (2002). We have never been modern. Cambridge, MA: Harvard University Press.

45   Lee, Z. (2014). Nurturing Communities of Inquiry in Philippine Schools. Thinking: The Journal of Philosophy for Children, 20(3), 76-82.
doi:10.5840/thinking2014203/411

46   Lipman, M., Sharp, A., & Oscanyan, F. (1980). Philosophy in the classroom (2nd ed.). Philadelphia: Temple University Press.

47   Lipman, M., & Montclair State College. (1974). Harry Stottlemeier's discovery Upper Montclair, N.J: Institute for the Advancement of Philosophy for Children, Montclair State College.

48   Lipman, M. (2003) Thinking in Education, 2nd edn. (Cambridge, Cambridge University Press).

49   Lofland, J., & Lofland, L. (1984). Analyzing Social Settings: A Guide to Qualitative Observation and Analysis. Belmont, CA: Wadsworth.

50   Lynch, M. P. (2008) "Alethic pluralism, logical consequence and the universality of reason," Midwest Studies in Philosophy, 32(1): 122–140.

51   Mates, B. (1961). Stoic logic. Berkeley: University of California Press.

52   McGinnis, N. D. (2013). The Unexpected Applicability of Paraconsistent Logic: AChomskyan Route to Dialetheism. Foundations Of Science, 18(4), 625-640.
doi:10.1007/s10699-012-9294-7

53   McNiff, J., & Whitehead, J. (2006). All you need to know about action research. London: SAGE.

54   Meyer, M. (2010). Abduction—A logical view for

investigating and initiating processes of discovering mathematical coherences. Educational Studies In Mathematics,
74(2), 185-205. doi:10.1007/s10649-010-9233-x

55   Morehouse, R. (1994) Cornel West and Prophetic Thought: Reflections on Community Within Community of Inquiry, Analytic Teaching, 15.1, pp. 41–44.

56   Moriyon, F. (2012). Promoting a Community of Scientific Inquiry [Review of journal Discussions in Science. Promoting conceptual understanding in the middle school years.]. Thinking: The Journal of Philosophy for Children, 94-96.

57   Nunes, T., Bryant, P., Evans, D., Bell, D., Gardner, S., Gardner, A., & Carraher, J.(2007). The contribution of logical reasoning to the learning of mathematics in primary school. British Journal Of Developmental Psychology, 25(1), 147-166. doi:10.1348/026151006X153127

58   Nussbaum, M. (2010) Not for Profit: Why Democracy Needs the Humanities (Princeton, NJ, Princeton University Press).

59   Peirce, C. S., Hartshorne, C., Weiss, P., & Burks, A. W. (1960). Collected papers of Charles Sanders Peirce. (Vol 5). Cambridge: Belknap Press of Harvard University Press

60   Peirce, C. S., Hartshorne, C., & Weiss, P. (1934). Collected papers. Cambridge: The Belknap Pr. of Harvard University Press.

61   Plato, ., & Fowler, H. N. (1961). Plato: Theaetetus, Sophist. London: Heinemann.

62   Raffman, D. (1994), "Vagueness Without Paradox", Philosophical Review 103: 41-74.

63   Restall, G. (2000) An Introduction to Substructural Logics, London: Routledge.

64   Restall, G. (2002) "Carnap's tolerance, language change and logical pluralism," Journal of Philosophy, 99: 426– 443.

170

65   Richards, J. L. (1980). The art and the science of British algebra: A study in the perception of mathematical truth. Historia Mathematica, doi:10.1016/0315-0860(80)90028-

66   Rowland, Tim. (2000). The Pragmatics of Education:Mathematical Discourse (Studies in Vagueness and Mathematics Education Series, 14). Taylor and Francis. Kindle Edition.

67   Russell, B.A.W. (1923) 'Vagueness', Australasian Journal of Psychology and Philosophy, 1, pp. 84–92.

68   Russell, G. (2008) "One true logic?" Journal of Philosophical Logic, 37(6): 593–611.

69   Russell, Gillian, "Logical Pluralism", The Stanford Encyclopedia of Philosophy (Winter 2016 Edition), Edward N. Zalta (ed.), URL =

<https://plato.stanford.edu/archives/win2016/entries/logical-pluralism/>.

70   Sainsbury, It. M. (1988), Paradoxes, Cambridge: Cambridge University Press.

71   Sainsbury, it. M. (1990), "Concepts Without Boundaries", Inaugural Lecture, published by the King's College London, Department of Philosophy;

72   Slade, C. (1997) Conversing Across Communities: Relativism and Difference, Analytic Teaching, 17.2, pp. 67–76.

73   Shapiro, S. (1997). Philosophy of mathematics structure and ontology. New York: Oxford University Press.

74   Shapiro, S. (2008). Vagueness in context. Oxford University Press.

75   Sharp, A. M. (1995) The Role of Intelligent Sympathy in Education for Global Consciousness, Critical and Creative Thinking, 3.2, pp. 13–37.

76   Sharp, A. M. (2009) The Child as Critic, in: E. Marsal, T. Dobashi and B. Weber (eds) Children Philosophize Worldwide: Theoretical and Practical Concepts (New York, Peter Lang).

77   Sprod, T. (1994). Developing higher order thinking through whole class discussion in a

science classroom. Unpublished masters dissertation, University of Oxford, Oxford.

78   Sprod, T. (1997a). Improving scientific reasoning through Philosophy for Children: An empirical study. Thinking 13 (2), 11-16.

79   Sprod, T. (1997b). 'Nobody really knows': The structure and analysis of social constructivist whole class discussion. International Journal of Science Education, 19 (8), 911-924.

80   Sprod, T. (1998). 'I can change your opinion on that': Social constructivist whole class discussion and their effect on scientific reasoning. Research in Science Education, 28, (4), 463-480.

81   Sprod, T. (2011). Discussions in science: Promoting conceptual understanding in the middle school years. Camberwell, Vic.: Australian Council for Educational Research.

82   Sutcliffe, R. (2014). Towards a Kinder Philosophy. Thinking: The Journal of Philosophy for Children, 20(3), 30-39. doi:10.5840/thinking2014203/46

83   Strauss, A., & Corbin, J. (1998). Basics of qualitative research: Techniques and procedures for developing grounded theory (2nd ed.). Thousand Oaks: Sage Publications.

84   Thomas, W., & Znaniecki, F. (1920). The Polish peasant in Europe and America: Monograph of an immigrant group. Boston: Richard G. Badger :.

85   Trickey, S., & Topping, K. J. (2004). 'Philosophy for children': A systematic review. Research Papers in Education, 19(3), 365-380. doi:10.1080/0267152042000248016

86   Tye, M. (1994). Sorites Paradoxes and the Semantics of Vagueness. Philosophical Perspectives, 8, 189. doi:10.2307/2214170

87   Ullmann, S. (1972). Semantics: An introduction to the science of meaning. Oxford: Blackwell.

172

88   van Benthem, J. (2008) "Logical dynamics meet logical pluralism?" The Australasian Journal of Logic, 6: 182–209.

89   Vansieleghem, N., & Kennedy, D. (2012). Philosophy for children in transition: Problems and prospects. Chichester, West Sussex: Wiley-Blackwell.

90   Vigliante, T. (2006) Effective Anti-Racism Education in Australian Schools: The Need for Philosophical Inquiry in Teacher Education, Critical and Creative Thinking: The Australasian Journal of Philosophy in Education, 13.1–2, pp. 90– 113.

91   Waismann, F. (1951b), "Analytic-Synthetic IV", Analysis 11: 115-24.

92   Weber, Z. (2010). A Paraconsistent Model of Vagueness. Mind, 119(476), 1025-1045.

93   Williamson, T. (1994). Vagueness. London   u.a.: Routledge.

94   Wittgenstein, L., Bosanquet, R., & Diamond, C. (1976). Lectures on the foundations of mathematics: Cambridge, 1939. Hassocks: Harvester.

95   Worrall, J. (1976). Boston studies in the philosophy of science (Vol. 39) (R. S. Cohen, R. J. Seeger, &M. W. Wartofsky, Eds.). Dordrecht, Holland: D. Reidel Publishing Company.

96   Wyatt, N. (2004) "What are Beall and Restall pluralists about?" Australasian Journal of `Philosophy, 82: 409–420.

Poetry by Andrew Nightingale

I would like the woods

If they had it on Facebook.
I would send an email to the sun, saying
"Thanks," or maybe
"Keep it up, and you'll have a bright future here at
World & Co."
I would teach the woods
To reach their full potential.
"Be positive, like the sun," I would say,
"Unless you have something better to
do." And the prophets would roll in With
their brand name coffee;
I would split profits in two,
One "in" and one "out" box.
I would; I have it all on my compose
screen, Waiting to send out.

—

Sex and Dearth

When I was young I could be among rocks.
Their mystery was solid,
Forming a hidden creation story.
In the beginning everything was

In the midsection, indifferent,
Now she is revealed,
Her solidity just another surface.
Oh to be among rocks again

– first published by AscentAspirations.com

Lets be birds in human bodies

We thought our sister had a boy's body
Her mind crawled inside a
chrysalis With her verb nouned.

"Lets suppose" says Socrates to Theaetetus, "That the mind is
an aviary,"
And Timaeus offers: "out of the innocent, light-
minded," Those with a clear sky for an aviary,
"Transformed into birds, and grew feathers instead of hair."

And missiles up in the air, as they are today,
Bring my sister flutters in her stomach.
She says they are real butterflies,
And that buzzing could be anything,
But for now it is still bees, they are asking us
To suppose our transmogration
Into a verb.

—

Yet another footprint on a world that needs nothing

I thought I was nobody without a home.
Nobody without a home
A foothold I could call my own, a place that would forever
accept my step
I wandered on blank sheets of paper.

I wanted to write about that piece of empty space
Dip the page in water, they say, and let the ink run by itself.
A paper vase where "animals drawn with a very fine
camelhair brush" could run alongside those "contained in the
present classification"
Turning the vase in my hands, the animals run, bleeding, until the
vase contains something.
(Write something into the vase)
The vase had writing curling round its inner walls, saying
"The truth is no-W-here."

I always wanted to work with wood, wood is good and
constructive, if temporary.
I wandered on blank sheets of paper
until I was accepted into the Hall of
Trees.

—

Pray

Bowstring bends the light
The Star-Hunter prays his line is taut enough.
(What prayer?)
Arrow streaks the night sky blue and gold
Finishing the game
As dawn peeks over the horizon to see
What prey?

—

Beauty is out to lunch

Around the corner
A dragon waits
For his tail to come 'round
So he can eat it.
The tail is you,
But if you stop looking
In the cupboards
And around the doors;
If you just sit down and wait,
You are the dragon.
I guess you won't be following this
Return.

See you around.

—

Great Change

Lightning on the mountain. Looking down,
On the map, roads cut rock all-at-once
Not like rivers, rivers stride
Like legless reptiles.

On the map, "You are here"
Over the rice fields, in the distance
The animals look like flies.
By river or road,
They quickly change to buffalo

(First published by PoetsHaven.com)

—

Birds of Tomorrow

When birds mate its just friends
Singing sweet nothings carelessly,
A wise gossip
Of travelled arcs written in the sky,
And sounding across the wide
Vision of clouds
On fire with a newborn sun.
They are not troubled by love.

—

Of death I have nothing to say

I was born screaming, I imagine
At the cold grip of air
Spilling out like a dishonored samurai
Into a room of sterile forms
The terror of open spaces, the chasms between moments
(Before I was one long budding moment)

But now I am not

The old man I dreamt I will be (please believe me, in a way)
I'm where I'm supposed to be, lying on a towel by a cement
pool with a woman who loves me
(She doesn't know me, and I won't tell)—
The sky is closed, the terrible pain in my heart.

—

How

In school I learned how white is black,
Have you ever seen a perfectly bright white?
A neutron star radiates out into blackness
The third dimension of light
Is matter in–
Forming and acting out.
What is the direction of light
Inside an electrified cloud of mercury and
fluorescence? To be clear, I mean "cloud" as in
"electron cloud."
A light that takes the color of all the
fluorescent Gods crowding up in this puta
madre.
I'd close my eyes and be ready to take my skin
off. Such a light would be closest to the ones
In cubicles who allow computer laws to rule out their lives,
Who, like angels, do not know the meaning of pain.

—

Blue Shell

If every rhyme were true,
How blue the sky would be;
How i would know i were me
And not a vessel for a crowd.
"Did you say a cloud?"
"That's your foggy cochlea speaking."
"White noise you mean?"
"Like the sound of the ocean,
Caught in our great blue shell."

—

Flicker

The world flickers
its daily show in the sun
And between the world and me
The rain falls
Sometimes you see it
Sometimes, times like today, you must dance between the flickers
So you always stay wet as water.
By pouring from one empty sunday to
another, The moment is always full

–(first published by Ascent Aspirations)

Farewell

My dog's name is dragon
And my dragon's name is
"Strange loop"
I'm thirty-five and I just realized
When I was a child my father told me
There were potatoes growing behind my ears
He didn't mean anything by it.
I was always asking
For the "innermost deepest meaning," so much
That the words became meaningless,
Much to my delight.
And I said to my daughter
That even if she couldn't fly,
Maybe her hair could.
I hope that wasn't too traumatic for her
There's another loon on the pond,
calling "Eureka!"
But all people hear is the madness in its voice.
Not chasing its tail, the loon
In that moment between air and water, leaps
It has to circle the pond to rise above the trees and
then Rising, God doesn't enter into it.

—

Pop Song Poem

That sound of the flute you can't grab on to
Makes the philosopher feel like a cave man, still
Banging rocks together.
The flute speaks to me
Long after it faded into wind
Long after
I stopped listening.

So many years have passed, but I remember
How much I lost to that sound.
Like breath in a winter fog,
Like tears in the rain,
Like wheels down an ever-winding
road, My heart empties, words slip
away.

—

Egg Poem

Oh, the possibilities of an egg
Which could be so many chickens
Who die and maybe are reborn
One as an antelope, or maybe a
baboon Then again, maybe not
Since I am eating the possibilities of this
egg Scrambled

And as I ate I tasted little
I was eating this poem instead

Sad to go on living this way
When all I can leave for you the
reader Is this empty basket of eggs.

181

—

Laughter is the wind
and jokes
the sailboats
waves of air rush towards stillness
and carry us
in the vacuum of their wake

—

Your time will come
One day, while you are
sleeping The sky will open up
The winds will swirl around you
Spiraling upwards in a giant funnel
And life will come pouring down into your backyard
Violent
Surging
Strange
You will be taken from your bed
You will go outside
And be washed.

—

Mourning

Floating to the edge of a still pond
that does not try to recollect What
reflected in passing Gone. Did the
sun die with me?
I wrap cold soaked fingers touching
blankets And we sit together sharing breath
Waiting
Watching the light-touched pond darken

—

Forgetting is for looking at the sky

"Latent" as Einstein called us:
The role of the common air.
What fills the empty spaces
        (ether? acting?)
Yet yields effortlessly
To all other occupations.
There is a hole in our zenith
No curvature to the wind
No essence of billowing clothes

No coincidence
As large as Archimedes' Axiom.

        —Always another atom further out there

Turning into a cloud, clouding us
        Cumulous

—

183
Gone

It's not the sounding of the gong,
Not the sudden silence that came before,
Or the drowning out of thoughts,
Making them whole with two-tones, no.

It's not the fading of the song.
It's when you're not sure you've lost it,
When you may have silence,
                    But you can't hear it.